MAGE OF THE HELLMOUTH

JOHN WAYNE COMUNALE

For the Coreys
May their hotline ring throughout the ages.

1

"HEY MAN, WAIT UP!"

Jake stepped out of his decade-old silver Civic with the dented front quarter panel to call out to his coworker, but Max was already walking up the steps to the loading dock and well out of earshot. The eternal, droning hum of the machines inside the Fam-Mark production facility made it hard to hear anything the closer you got to the building.

Jake and Max had long ago fallen into the routine of smoking a bowl before their shift every morning. Jake worked at Fam-Mark longer than Max but only by a couple of months, and the two bonded over a shared affinity for marijuana. Of course, the company didn't particularly like employees to get stoned before operating heavy machinery, but if the higher-ups ever worked one day on the production line, they'd realize just how necessary the pre-work ritual was.

The two watched out for each other and had the other's back when their production manager, Rob, gave them shit, which was pretty much always. Rob was an uptight, ultra-fastidious guy who was always at maximum stress level regardless of the situation. Any information he had to deliver was always of utmost importance, requiring the undivided attention of those on shift to the extent Rob would pull people off the line one at a time to tell it to them.

Since he acted as if every single thing was an emergency and should be treated as such, Jake, Max, and the other Fam-Mark employees soon realized nothing was an *actual* emergency. This significantly lessened the impact of any direction he gave, prompting many to ignore what their supervisor said about anything. Aside from Rob's overbearing, idiosyncratic behavior he was forever sweating, even before he'd done any work. Jake had seen the man arrive with his shirt already beginning to show signs of perspiration slowly spreading out from under his arms. How a person could sweat so much while spending the majority of their day in a freezing production room was a mystery to Jake and the rest of Rob's subordinates.

Fam-Mark made ice cream, but not just any ice cream. They made what was referred to as "craft ice cream," or "craft-cream" depending on how pretentious the person referring to it was. Fam-Mark infused unique flavors into their confections to create a countless number of combinations such as rosewater-cucumber-yam and apple-curry-walnut.

Jake wasn't familiar with the entire selection of flavors because those were made at a separate Fam-Mark facility on the east side of town. Where he and Max worked, they only made the gluten-free, dairy-free, and, for the most part, flavor-free line of ice creams. These "alternative" varieties had to be produced in an entirely separate facility to guarantee absolutely no cross-contamination because, while some people break out in hives when they eat something they're allergic to, other people die.

Jake went to the main facility once for a training meeting and found it unsettling. He couldn't decide why he felt that way. The building was easily triple the size or more and, while the amount of cars in the parking lot suggested a small army of employees, Jake didn't see any extraneous people roaming the halls. The larger facility churned out more product in a day than Jake's could in two weeks so he couldn't imagine every employee would be busy at the same time, but he'd been wrong before.

The market for Fam-Mark's line of dietary-restriction-friendly ice cream was considerably small, hence the smaller facility and staff. It wasn't just the size Jake didn't like about the sister facility; there were other things too.

The machines were so different from what he was used to they may as well have been a form of advanced alien technology. The production line and conveyor belts moved in a very different way he found disorienting to look at for more then a few seconds. Something about the combined motion of the workers and machines gave Jake the creeps and, while he didn't get a long enough look to tell for sure, the entire line appeared to defy the laws of physics.

The other thing Jake didn't like about the bigger facility was the general sense of unease he felt while there. He dismissed it initially as mild anxiety brought on from being in an unfamiliar space but, as the day went by, he realized it was something else entirely.

The place gave Jake the creeps, and he couldn't stifle a bout of involuntary shivering until the main facility was a dot in his rearview mirror. Needless to say, the facility where he worked had its share of hassles and annoying idiosyncrasies, but they were nothing compared to what Jake could imagine went on over there.

What he liked best about the small facility was the crew because it made everyone who worked there a little tighter than they would be if the group were larger. This also meant you knew where you stood with everyone, which regulated the amount and importance of information shared with certain people. Everyone was cool for the most part, but Jake could see through the fakeness some of his fellow employees put on when it suited them.

Aside from their appreciation for potent marijuana, Jake and Max bonded over a disdain for the disingenuous poseurs who walked amongst them daily. They spent many morning smoke sessions doing caricature-like impressions of how certain co-workers would act when Rob was nearby, including the individual affectations they applied to their tone and cadence. Jake and Max talked to Rob the same way they would talk to each other or anyone else they interacted with and, while it mostly annoyed their supervisor, Jake believed, deep down, he respected them for it.

Jake ducked back into the Civic, took a few quick puffs on the bowl he'd intended on sharing with his friend, and began gathering what he needed for the day. The required lab coats were provided by Fam-Mark but did little to protect against the freezing temperatures of the production room they spent hours at a time working in. Jake brought a long-sleeve t-shirt, a hoodie, facemask, and a black knit hat along with his *Dawn of the Dead* lunchbox, which usually contained two tallboy cans of whatever beer was on sale that week along with a granola bar or two. Jake got the lunchbox at a horror convention three years ago and started using it to actually carry his lunch in when he started working at Fam-Mark.

According to the digital clock on his dashboard, Jake was nine minutes late, but he still sauntered slowly through the small parking lot as if he had arrived with time to spare. Sometimes Jake and Max would sit in the Civic smoking until fifteen or twenty minutes after the designated start time of seven a.m., which made Jake wonder why Max seemed to be in such a hurry to get to work. His languid meandering ate up several more minutes, and when he pulled open the door to the facility the clock on the wall across from him read 7:17.

As strict as Rob was, he gave a thirty-minute grace period in the morning for being late. Some of the crew drove in from suburbs on the fringe of the city and, with traffic in the area being unpredictable, the production manager was lenient to an extent.

Thirty minutes was where it ended though because anyone arriving even one minute later was issued a written warning for tardiness. Three written warnings for the same offense was grounds for immediate termination. Everyone on the crew believed Rob would do it because he'd fired people in front of everyone multiple times. Everyone figured he did it to show he wasn't making idle threats and, as much as it sucked, it was another example of knowing where you stood with everyone, Rob included.

Jake yawned as he tossed his lunchbox onto one of the shelves of the refrigerator in what Fam-Mark deemed was an acceptable space for an employee break room. It was small and felt cramped when three people occupied it at once, which was just as well because the single table pushed against the wall only had two chairs shoved beneath it.

No one ate in the break room except for new people who hadn't figured it out yet, but it didn't take them long. Some people would sit outside dangling their legs from the loading dock to warm up from being in a thirty-three-degree room all morning with most of them spending the short reprieve from work bitching about the things they hated about the work itself.

Jake and Max found those particular employees' behavior counterproductive and chose not to spend their lunch break fraternizing with them. The two would climb into Jake's Civic to drive down the block to the back of a grocery store parking lot.

They would smoke some more and sip the beers Jake brought until Max would inevitably end up walking into the store to buy two more cold tallboys for them to chug before heading back to the facility.

Jake yawned again as he rounded the corner to where a wall lined with pegs was designated for employees to hang their bags and extra sweaters or coats. Seven was a lot earlier than Jake would have liked to start working, but he knew it could be worse. They ran the *other* Fam-Mark twenty-four hours a day, with some shifts starting at 2 a.m., which he would have a much harder time with.

He expected to find Max in the hall, but there was no sign of him. After Jake suited up in his layers and put his lab coat on, he headed toward the production room to check the schedule for what position he'd be working that day when Max came around the corner.

"Whoa, watch where you're going there, buddy," Jake said in a mocking tone he and Max often spoke to each other almost exclusively with. "If you run into me and I get hurt I won't get workman's comp because I can't pass the drug test. You know that. By the way, why were you in such a hurry to get inside today?"

"Sorry, man," Max managed weakly. "I don't feel so good today for some reason."

Jake was about to respond with an off-color joke involving his mother and a sex-act being the reason Max was sick, but he held back when he realized how bad his friend looked. This clearly wasn't the usual hangover, and if Max had planned to fake sick, he would have included Jake so they could fuck-off all day together.

"Oh shit," Jake said, speaking in his normal voice now. "You're not bullshitting either, huh? You look pretty fucking sick, dude."

The color was gone from Max's face and his skin looked thin and fragile, almost translucent. He stood with his shoulders hunched forward like he was going to curl up into a ball and roll away. Jake had never seen Max look like this.

"No shit," Max replied. "I just shit and puked my guts out. Rob was standing outside of the bathroom waiting for me to come out to tell me to go home. He said I was putting the entire facility at risk by being here a minute longer."

"What a creepy perv," Jake quipped. "I bet he was getting turned on listening to you shit your guts out."

"Probably." Max managed a soft laugh, though his expression quickly changed. He was obviously in pain.

"Can you drive home?" Jake asked, mostly out of concern, but also hoping to score extra time away from the facility helping get his friend home safely.

"I already called Paris from Rob's office. She's on her way to pick me up."

Paris was Max's sister who he was very close to. They were barely a year apart and had formed some unusually strong familial bond free of hatred and resentment. It was baffling to Jake how Max and his sister got along so well, but he didn't mind her being around since she was pretty cool as far as he was concerned.

Jake had started to develop a tiny crush on his friend's sister but tried not to think about it. He hoped it didn't develop into something he'd want to end up pursuing since starting a relationship with her would more than upset the applecart of his life. It could seriously damage or alter his relationship with Max, or end the friendship completely.

There were many potential, tangential offshoots of what dating Max's sister could or would do to Jake's life, with varying degrees of awfulness. They all ended with the two of them having to work together every day whether they liked it or not. Jake preferred they "like" it and swore to himself he'd do his best to *keep it in his pants*—so-to-speak—when it came to Paris.

"Okay, man." Jake pulled his shirt up to cover his nose as if Max had the plague. "Get out of here, and go get better. You seriously look like total shit."

"Ha-ha, thanks."

Max faux laughed as he continued past Jake on his way out of the facility. He turned the corner before continuing to the production room. He was just giving his friend a hard time, but Max really did look bad. Jake hoped it wasn't anything serious and, even more so, hoped he hadn't contracted the illness himself. He and Max spent a lot of time together and smoked from the same pipe several times daily.

"Jake, I need to see you in my office."

Rob's voice came from behind, startling him on multiple levels. First, it surprised him, for sure. Also, he had just turned around from talking to Max and hadn't seen Rob coming down the hall. Rob was a sneaky bastard but was he *that* slick?

"Yes, oh captain, my captain." Jake turned to see his supervisor frowning, hands on his hips.

"Just shut up and get in there." Rob wasn't in the mood to play games this morning. He never was, regardless of the time of day.

2

ROB'S OFFICE WAS EVEN WORSE than the employee break room. It was too small to accommodate an actual desk, so instead he used a small, round, café-style table salvaged from a cafeteria makeover from back in the eighties. A phone perched on the right side of the makeshift desk while the rest of the space was littered with papers. Instead of file cabinets there were three orange, plastic milk crates against the back wall. Not stacked. Side by side.

They were stuffed with manila folders containing information pertinent to his position, but Jake had no idea what his supervisor kept track of. The folders weren't in alphabetical order, or sequentially sorted, but were instead arranged in a way that made sense only to Rob. They were his files, and he used *his* system. This was an example of one of the many behaviors Jake, Max, and most of the other employees found annoying about their boss.

Rob entered the room first and walked around to the other side of the table, but didn't sit down. Jake stepped in and sat at the chair opposite his boss, waiting to see what it was that had Rob so worked up. He laughed to himself at the thought of the production manager listening to Max shit outside the bathroom door like he was overhearing him confess to murder and waiting until he came out so he could throw the book at him.

Jake looked up at Rob standing across the table from him and noticed the man was genuinely rattled. He was sweating, of course, which was nothing new, but the expression on his face cast a different light on Rob's perspiration. His mouth was closed and pulled tight across his face in a straight line, making his lips non-existent.

The production manager's eyes were squinty, matching the line of his mouth running parallel to it like the curb on either side of the street. Also, Jake noticed Rob was far too damp with sweat for this early in the day, even for him.

His hair stuck to the back of his neck in slick, greasy, matted tufts like the oil-covered tentacles of a battle-weary octopus. The collar of his white shirt was yellow and wilted, and his tie tried desperately to stay in place by clinging to the moist, slippery fabric with little luck. The dampness loosened the knot of the colorful noose to show the already undone top button of Rob's shirt.

For a second Jake was starting to think something might actually be wrong. He flashed to the image of passing his sickly best friend in the hall and had a sudden rush of anxiety thinking Rob was going to tell him Max's condition was something serious.

"Hey, Rob, wha—"

The shrill and jarring ring of the phone cut Jake off, and he felt the vibration through his hand, only now realizing he'd grabbed the table. Rob's hand shot to the receiver and ripped it from the cradle like a viper striking to snatch up its prey. Jake noticed a fine mist of sweat spring from the top of his hand the moment it made impact with phone, dotting the papers next to it with tiny, moist droplets.

"Yes," Rob said, turning from his desk, the worn, coiled cord stretching tight across his love handles.

Jake, still clutching the table, sat up in his chair and leaned forward, trying to hear, but Rob was doing a good job of muffling the short, staccato replies to whatever was being said to him on the other line. Rob absently ran the hand he wasn't holding the phone with back through his hair, and it stuck to his scalp like it was full of pomade. Jake wasn't able to move his hand fast enough to avoid being struck with several drops of the torrential downpour of perspiration springing from the oversaturated hair.

Jake shook the sweat from his hand before vigorously rubbing it against his jeans, hoping the denim was coarse enough to remove the top layer of his skin. He suddenly felt something wet roll down the side of his face and thought he'd been struck by another errant sweat bead. He brought his hand to his face to wipe it away and realized it belonged to him.

He'd suited up in all his layers—lab coat included—in preparation to walk directly into the freezing production room and had not anticipated taking an excursion into Rob's office. His clothes suddenly felt constrictive and too tight, like they were all shrinking at the same time.

A layer of moisture pushed its way from Jake's pores to dampen the fabric of his jeans and the t-shirt he wore as the foundation for his cold-weather gear. The moistened fabric felt prickly and itchy, like angry ants were trapped beneath and were angrily trying to bite their way to freedom through his many layers.

Jake unbuttoned his lab coat and scratched his chest, suddenly finding it unbearable to spend one more second with his clothes on. Rob dropped the receiver back to the cradle, which snapped Jake from his tension-fueled anxiety attack. He was still sweating beneath the stifling heat of his layers, but he no longer felt the urge to disrobe completely right there in Rob's office.

One more second of silence passed between the two, their eyes locked. For a single moment, the men shared the same pang of fear, but for different reasons.

"They're shutting us down," Rob said plainly.

A drop of sweat clinging to the tip of his nose let go and landed next to a puddle made up of the lemmings before it.

"They're shu—"

"Yes," Rob interrupted. He was doing his best to maintain the usual stern tone he gave direction in, but a slight waiver sneaked through. "Due to fluctuating changes in the marketplace, Fam-Mark has decided to discontinue its line of products that cater to specific dietary restrictions."

Rob was speaking with the emotional cadence of a text-to-speech app, making the cold, impersonal words somehow even more clinical and foreign. It was like he was reciting sounds he'd rehearsed that included instructions on when and where to add emphasis but was still unsure of their meaning.

The odd delivery confused Jake further, making it harder to understand what Rob was saying and allowing it to fully sink in, but then, all at once, it did. He was losing his job.

"So, I'm fired? We're all fired?"

"No, not exactly," Rob said. He'd started pacing in the small amount of room on the far side of the table. "No one is being *fired*, but some people will be *laid-off*."

"What's the difference? It means the same thing."

Jake's mind was already racing with ideas of where he could apply for other jobs that were on the way back to his apartment. He was able to eliminate ninety percent of them right away, knowing they'd require a drug test he wouldn't be able to pass for several weeks. The remaining ten percent were less than desirable, consisting mostly of gas stations and restaurants. Jake flashed forward to scenarios in which he was forced to work a number of shitty, name-tag wearing jobs until he could find another gig as easygoing as the Fam-Mark facility.

"It means," Rob said, gritting his teeth, derailing Jake's train of thought, "that some people won't have a job anymore, and another small percentage of employees will be transferred to the main Fam-Mark facility across town. Of course, it is completely up to those chosen whether or not they'd like to remain with the company, or leave to seek work elsewhere."

The shock was wearing off, and Jake was now able to understand what was happening. He wasn't losing his job. Why would Rob give him all this background if he were among those being *laid off?*

"So, which group do I fall in?" Jake knew the answer, but asked the question anyway. Rob waited another moment before replying.

"Jake," he began, "you are among those who will be transferred to the main facility. If you choose to accept this offer, you'll begin there tomorrow."

"Wow, that soon? Isn't there still work to do here? Aren't there still orders that need to be filled?"

"The company has ceased all production as of yesterday, and all customer orders have been canceled through the distribution centers."

"But I hear the machines running now?"

"The manufacturers sent a maintenance crew earlier this morning. They're running a chemical cleaning flush through everything before they start to dismantle and remove the equipment. There's no more product being made in the production rooms."

Jake was stunned by the sheer quickness with which things were moving, but he supposed when a company, especially a smaller one like Fam-Mark, needed to make cuts to save money, they were immediate and indiscriminate.

"So," Rob placed his hands flat on the table and looked down at Jake while the avalanche of sweat continued tumbling off the slope of the supervisor's forehead. "are you going to accept the transfer and remain part of the Fam-Mark family?"

3

JAKE LAY IN BED STARING up into the languidly dissipating cloud of marijuana smoke as he gently pushed it from his lungs and out past his lips. The Roky Erickson record he'd been listening to ended several minutes ago. The needle bumped up against the label as it continued to spin soundlessly. He was stoned and lost in thought and had yet to get up to flip the record over.

The entire day felt surreal, and the news he received from Ron was jarring. Jake had felt something off since that morning when Max missed their pre-work smoking ritual because he'd supposedly been ill. Supposedly? He saw Max before he left, and he looked sicker than Jake had ever seen anyone look outside of a zombie movie.

Any other day Jake would never have second-guessed the validity of Max's ailment, but this particular day left him questioning everything. He knew he was stoned at the moment, but Jake had begun to deeply consider the possibility he'd accidentally stumbled into another iteration of his usual reality where everything was sort of the same, but not quite.

He'd accepted the transfer to the main Fam-Mark facility despite every fiber of his being teaming together to rally against the decision. When Rob told him about the raise it was a no-brainer. Jake had been literally trying to decide what menial service industry job to apply for, which was where he would much rather work than the other facility, but a five dollar an hour raise was too much to turn down.

Rob had almost forgotten to mention the raise, treating it as an afterthought, having assumed Jake was already aware of it. Taking the transfer wasn't ideal for him, but it meant he would be making significantly more money than he was currently, or ever had in his life.

Images flashed through Jake's head of the benefits having more income could afford him, including a new or, at the very least, newer car. He would be able to buy more weed at a time and even splurge on some of the craft beers he'd been wanting to try but was dissuaded by the price. He could finally upgrade his stereo and get rid of the piece of shit receiver and semi-blown speakers.

Jake rested his pipe on the nightstand and rolled out of bed. Thinking about new stereo components reminded him to get up and flip the record. He dropped the needle just beyond the first groove and the song "Two-Headed Dog" sprang from the speakers in the middle of the opening riff. Jake returned to his bed, snatching the pipe up as he rolled back atop the rumpled tangle of sheets. He took another long, slow drag and let the smoke tingle his lungs before releasing it through his nostrils.

After telling Rob he would accept the offer to transfer, Jake immediately thought of his friend and wanted to know if Max was among the transferred.

"It's against company policy to divulge personal information about employees to anyone including other employees."

Rob had rattled off the answer like it had been cued up in his head for a while, and he'd been itching to pull the trigger.

"Come on," Jake had said. "Just tell me. You know Max is pretty much my best friend, so he's going to tell me anyway. I could probably still catch him out front right now and ask, so just let me know."

"If you want to know so bad then you can run to try and catch him," Rob said, trying to fight the edges of his mouth from turning up slightly. He'd gotten enjoyment out of enforcing the small amount of power he still had left over Jake.

"Okay, whatever." Jake had waved dismissively. "Well, are *you* a member of the transferred, chosen ones?"

Jake's tone was like that of a petulant child, but the sudden— albeit slight—change in Rob's expression had given him his answer.

"It has yet to be determined which members of management will be transferred, but I assure you that is none of your concern."

"Oh, I'm not concerned about it."

Jake had then stood, removed his lab coat, and let it fall to the chair behind him.

"So, is that it then? I take it there's no work here to do since the machines are being cleaned and dismantled." Jake had been in a hurry, hoping he could still catch Max to see if he was transferring as well.

"That's all for now," Rob had replied, sitting in the chair he'd been standing behind. "Report to the main facility tomorrow at six a.m. sharp. Someone should be there to meet all the transferees, give you the lay of the land, and assign you to your new job."

"Are you sure I have to start tomorrow?"

The thought of having to be at the main facility in less than twenty-four hours had hung heavy in his head like oversaturated storm clouds ready to drop more than enough rain to ruin anybody's day.

"Yes, tomorrow." Rob ran the back of his hand across his forehead, but it had only made him sweatier. "Might I remind you that the majority of your co-workers will *not* have a job to go to tomorrow, let alone in a few days."

Rob had huffed and turned his attention to his desk where he started shuffling papers, leaving wavy, wet fingermarks everywhere he touched. Jake had known arguing wouldn't get him anywhere, and he'd still wanted to see if he could catch up to Max before Paris picked him up. He almost had said goodbye to his supervisor, not knowing if he'd ever see him again, but decided he didn't really care and left the office without saying anything.

Now, Jake took another hit from his pipe, but didn't pull too hard since the bowl was close to being cashed. He rolled over, sat on the side of his bed while exhaling, and placed the pipe back on the nightstand next to the telephone he'd had since high school. It was the kind where the receiver and the base were made of clear plastic so the guts of the phone were visible, and there were a few surreptitiously placed tiny light bulbs within that flashed every time it rang.

The lights hadn't worked for some time, but the phone itself still did so Jake never thought to get rid of it. Sometimes it was hard for him to believe it had actually been ten years since he graduated from high school but, believe it or not, the time had blazed by. The only thing he still owned from that time in his life was the half-broken telephone he was staring at, willing it to ring.

By the time he'd gotten from Rob's office to the front of the facility, Max was gone. When Jake got back to his apartment he tried calling but got the answering machine. Max and Paris split an apartment that wasn't very far from the facility, so they would have beat Jake home, especially with the head start. Also, Jake had taken a longer way back to his place, drinking his lunch beers and thinking about his talk with Rob as he went.

He'd figured Max wasn't home because Paris had taken him to the doctor, or they'd stopped to get medicine from a pharmacy, but hours had gone by and Jake didn't hear back from them. He'd left two messages, the latest being almost three hours ago. He stopped trying to call altogether an hour ago when the machine picked up yet again.

It was starting to get dark. Jake walked over to his bedroom window. He opened it halfway to let the stale reefer smoke out and the cool evening breeze in. He'd left a beer on the windowsill earlier in the afternoon. It was warm but still half-full. He sipped the tepid longneck as he looked out his window through bleary, red eyes. He'd started to think about the best route to take in the morning, but wasn't sure what traffic was like going to the other side of town that early in the morning.

Jake's apartment was on the second floor, but his view was unobstructed from the bedroom window, giving him a clear of view across the river of the town. He stared out at it, pretending he could actually see the roads he'd be traversing in the morning, but it was no use. He'd have to take a chance and hope it worked out for the best until he could ascertain the quickest and least trafficked route.

He was pretty sure he remembered the direction the main Fam-Mark facility was in, but it was too far to see from Jake's apartment. Or was it? He blinked several times, trying to work moisture back into his eyeballs, hoping he was mistaken, but he could still see it. It was so glaringly apparent in the dark Jake didn't know how he hadn't seen it before.

He was looking in the direction of the Fam-Mark facility and, while the actual building wasn't visible, he could see a pale-pink light radiating up from the far side of town. The light hung in the air just above the spot he was looking at, and tiny wisps of pink floated off the light like strands of cotton candy stretched until they didn't exist anymore. Jake turned away and thought about going up to the roof for a better look when his phone rang.

4

A VERY TIRED SOUNDING PARIS apologized to Jake for not being able to get back to him and appreciated his concern for Max, but her tone wrapped the sentiment in a thin layer of annoyance. She said she'd taken Max to a local clinic and, when they examined him, he was so dehydrated Paris was told to immediately take him to the hospital. They didn't have the intravenous equipment there required to rehydrate Max, so she loaded him back in the car and headed to the hospital.

Jake remembered how pale Max looked that morning, and how he'd said he was puking and shitting and couldn't stop. He'd never known Max to be a big water drinker, so Jake could see how it would be easy for his friend to become dehydrated much faster than someone who took better care of themselves. Still, Max had been fine the day before and didn't mention anything about starting to feel sick.

He knew some viruses could come on in an instant and, possibly, on his way home from work, Max touched the wrong door handle or shook the wrong hand. The microscopic parasite more than likely spread its infection while Max slept and, once awake, what remained of his health deteriorated quickly while the virus continued to gorge itself.

Jake knew he had to be at least partially right. Otherwise he would be as sick since they'd both smoked from the same pipe several times and were, in fact, the *only* people to smoke from it all day. Jake was in worse shape than Max, especially when it came to what he put in his body, subsisting primarily on fast food burritos and an assortment of food-based substances requiring no effort to prepare.

It was obvious to Jake that Paris didn't want to be on the phone any longer than necessary, and she didn't hide the frustration in her voice when he started asking questions.

"Hey, did Max say anything to you about the facility closing?"

Jake pushed the words out too quickly and each one started on the heels of the one before it.

"What?"

Jake was pretty sure he heard Paris yawn after asking the question.

"No, he didn't," she continued, "but he really didn't say much of anything. All he could do was moan after I picked him up, and whatever they gave him at the hospital has him out cold."

"Really?" Jake immediately felt guilty for being incensed at his friend for being too sick to properly communicate. He started again, "I mean, Rob took me to his office to tell me the facility was closing as of today and that some of us were being transferred to the main facility across town."

"What about the people they aren't transferring?"

"What do you think? That's why I wanted to see if Max said anything about being transferred or not. That prick Rob said he couldn't legally divulge the information, or some shit."

Three seconds of silence passed before Paris said anything again, and Jake thought they might have gotten disconnected.

"Hello? Paris, are you there?"

"Yeah, I'm here," she finally said. "I thought I heard Max moaning again, but I guess it was nothing."

The fatigue in her voice had become twice as heavy since the conversation started, and Jake could feel the weight pushing against his ear through the receiver.

"Okay," he began. "Don't worry about it. Just take care of Max."

"I'll put a note by his bed for him to call you when he wakes up."

"Thanks." Jake should have hung up right then, but his mouth acted faster than his common sense. "And Paris, make sure to take care of yourself too."

He'd said it with a rehearsed, false intimacy without realizing how lame the words would sound until he heard it himself. Paris hung up without a reply, and he hoped she'd disconnected before his bumbled flirting attempt, but he knew she hadn't.

He hung up the phone and slowly made his way back over to the window, bringing his pipe with him this time. He put it to his lips and took a hit while looking back across the river at the city, doing his best to ignore the pink glow, but his eyes were drawn to it again and again.

The constrictive pressure of Jake's anxiety had loosened some upon hearing that Max was at least doing better, but the news wasn't enough to abate it fully. He hoped to hear from Max before morning but knew the chances were slim. Transferred or not, Jake knew his friend wouldn't be well enough to start a new job the day after being so ill anyway.

Jake was going to have to face his first day at the new facility on his own.

5

THE NEXT MORNING, JAKE WAITED as long as possible for Max's call, but he didn't want to be late for his first day at the main facility. He might have been able to play fast and loose with being late before, but he had no idea if they were as forgiving as Rob had been regarding tardiness.

He almost called again in the final moments before he left but stopped before he finished dialing. It was early, and Max was sick. Calling now would only wake up Paris, and Jake didn't want to piss her off any more. There were bound to be phones at the new facility available for employee use, so he could try to call during lunch. Maybe he'd consider getting a cell phone with his new raise.

As Jake stepped out the door while slipping on his jacket, he realized a call at lunch might not be necessary after all. Rob told him there would be someone waiting at the facility to meet the transfers and show them around, or something like that. This person would no doubt have a list of everyone's name they were supposed to meet. If they took roll and Max's name wasn't called, Jake would have his answer.

Jake pulled into the parking lot of the main Fam-Mark facility with six minutes to spare. The lot was much bigger than he remembered, and he found a space down the first row close to the back. He gathered his things quickly, and started to walk toward the entrance at a brisk pace. He didn't smoke on the way to work that morning so the smell wouldn't follow him in and he figured he might as well be straight for at least the first half of the day until he got comfortable with what he was doing.

He remembered the machines he'd seen the other time he'd been there and how foreign they looked. He knew it wouldn't take more than a day or two before operating the odd-looking equipment became commonplace for him, but the machines did have an otherworldly aesthetic that made Jake nervous.

One of the reasons he liked his job so much was how easy it was, allowing him to check out mentally. He worried working the machines here would require he pay closer attention, thereby making it nearly impossible to maintain a buzz no matter how high he got. Jake stopped himself from exploring that mode of thought any further since he really had no idea what his new position would entail and speculating wasn't doing him any good.

"It's gonna be fine," he said to himself. "It's gonna be just fine."

Jake believed what he said, or convinced himself he did for the time being. As he approached the facility, Jake found he missed Max a little more than he had before he got out of the car.

Jake couldn't see through the mirrored doors but took advantage of the reflection to fix his hair before pulling on the handle. He didn't realize a woman stood behind the door and it noticeably startled him. He jumped back a step and dropped his hoodie before immediately becoming flush with embarrassment.

"S-Sorry," he stuttered as he picked up his things and tried to recover.

The woman simply nodded in reply before bringing the clipboard she held up to eyelevel. She had straight black hair to her shoulders, round-frame glasses, and a narrow face. Jake thought she wore a white dress until he noticed she was already wearing a lab coat. He suddenly realized the woman bore a striking resemblance to The Baroness from G.I. Joe.

Jake owned the toy of the character as a kid along with a hundred or so other action figures from the line. The Baroness was one of the few female characters in the G.I. Joe universe, and the fact she was a "bad guy" made her the most appealing by far. Being clad from head to toe in a skintight, leather suit didn't hurt either.

"Are you Jacob Bowman?"

The woman's voice was toneless and lacked warmth, making his own name sound foreign to him.

"That's me. I mean, yes, but you can call me Jake."

He stumbled again and felt his face get hotter as even more blood flooded the vessels in his face. The woman didn't seem to notice and, in fact, wasn't even looking at Jake. Her eyes remained on the clipboard as she removed a pen attached at the top and used it to mark a check on whatever was clipped to the other side.

"Follow me."

The woman turned on her heels and started down a hallway at a brisk pace. Jake stood at the door confused for a moment before having to jog to catch up to her.

"Aren't we going to wait for the others?" Jake called as he closed the gap between them. "You know, the rest of the transfers?"

"There are no others," she replied without looking back or breaking stride.

Jake stopped, now certain he'd misheard, and called after her.

"Wait, what?"

"You're the only one on the list."

Jake stopped and watched the woman disappear between swinging, red doors separating the hall from another section of the facility, too stunned to follow.

6

JAKE SAT IN THE DARK conference room alone while a video he was supposed to be watching played on a television strapped to a cart at the front of the room. The woman he'd been following had started the video and told him she'd be back when it was over. She'd explained what purpose the video served as he followed her to the room, but he hadn't been paying attention.

How could he after she told him he was the only person who'd been transferred to the facility? It had to be a misunderstanding. She probably meant he was the only one on *her* list. It seemed inefficient to train and orient the transfers one by one, but what did he know? Maybe it had something to do with Fam-Mark's insurance on the facility.

Jake could imagine there being a clause in their policy requiring all employees be trained one at a time for some kind of corporate safety measure. It was a stretch but it was the only way he could make sense of the situation. He couldn't accept being the only transfer from the other facility as truth.

The television displayed a sweeping camera shot across the top of a machine Jake guessed he was supposed to be learning something from. Nothing about how the stainless-steel pieces fit together made sense to Jake and resembled something more suited for the space program or a science-fiction novel. If there was a voice-over explaining what he was looking at, he wasn't paying attention to that either.

He kept telling himself over and over that this was a misunderstanding. Jake imagined, on either side of him, identical conference rooms where other transfers solitarily viewed the same video, just as confused by it as he was.

He figured once the training was done they would all be gathered together and be given their assigned position for the day. Of course, Max wouldn't be there either way, but maybe one of the people from his old facility knew something Jake didn't. Jake snapped from his thoughts when the lights suddenly came on. He didn't notice the video had finished.

The woman's shoes clacked loudly against the tile as she walked up the aisle and past Jake to the front of the room. She pushed a button on the television and the static shrunk to a tiny dot of light in the center of the screen where it held for just a moment before fading away.

"Any questions Mister . . ." She held the clipboard up and read his last name like it all of a sudden became difficult to pronounce. "Bowman?"

"You can call me Jake," he replied quickly. "And, yes, I do have a question."

She gave no verbal response and instead waited in silence for him to ask, heightening the uncomfortable awkwardness.

"First of all," Jake started, "what's your name?"

The woman's expression told Jake his question "did not compute."

"I mean," he stumbled, trying to backpedal out of any creepy vibe he might have put out. "I like to know the names of people I work with, and I just realized you know my name but I don't know yours."

"My name is Elise, and we will not be working together, Mr. Bowman. Do you have a question regarding the information in the video you watched?"

The tone of her voice alone was enough to lower the temperature of the room by twenty degrees, and Jake cringed against the chill as he tried another approach.

"Nope," he smiled. "I'm all good on that. Shipshape."

"Then please follow m—"

"You know what?" Jake cut Elise off. "I actually have another question about what we were talking about earlier."

Elise crossed her arms and narrowed her eyes.

"And what *were* we talking about earlier?"

"The whole transfer thing we talked about when I first got here.

Remember?"

She stared silently, again waiting for him to continue, but he picked up on it quickly this time and kept talking.

"I think I misunderstood when you said I was the *only* transfer from the other facility because I'm sure you meant I was the only transfer you were training, right?"

"I'm afraid that's confidential employee information and it cannot be divulged to you."

Her answer made him suddenly remember his old boss.

"What about Rob?" In his excitement he'd inadvertently raised his voice but caught himself and corrected it quickly. "I mean, what about management? Rob was my old supervisor. Did he make the cut?"

Elise stared and said nothing, but this time Jake knew she wasn't waiting for him to continue. The silence had answered his question.

"Mr. Bowman, if you don't have any questions about the video, please follow me."

She started for the door without giving him time to ask another question regardless whether it pertained to the video or not. Jake got the distinct sense he'd used up all the question time Elise allotted and stood slowly, following in line behind her. He didn't remember a thing about the video and didn't particularly care.

Jake felt alone, and he didn't like it. Not only was Max apparently very ill, he still had no idea if he was going to be working at the facility with him. He briefly considered the idea of meeting new people, as daunting as it was exciting, but Jake had a feeling it was going to be different at the new facility. He'd only met Elise and, while she assured him they would *not* be working together, he couldn't help thinking everyone else who worked there would somehow mimic her frigidly aggressive unapproachability.

Jake knew it was an overly dramatic idea. There was no possible way *everyone* else who worked at the facility was as "warm" as his orientation leader. In his logical mind Jake knew he was overreacting. Once he got over the shock of being transferred, he could settle into his temporary role as the "new guy" until he was able to ingratiate himself to his coworkers.

He knew everything would be fine. If Max wasn't joining him, they could still hang out after work and on weekends when they were both free. In fact, when considering his routes to and from the facility, he discovered one that would take him right by Max and

Paris's apartment on his way home.

Jake's entire thought process was a legitimately logical order of operations for how his first few weeks at work would be and, although it made perfect sense, he wasn't convinced. Something felt off about everything since he'd arrived, from his first impressions of Elise to the sanitary drabness of the hallways, oddly silent for a building where many large machines were operating at once.

He realized he'd either slowed his pace or Elise had quickened hers because he was now a good six feet behind her. As he stepped up to lessen the distance, Jake noticed something he hadn't earlier. He might not have seen it now if the light hadn't momentarily glinted off the thing.

As Elise walked, she held the clipboard to her chest with one arm while the other swung slightly by her side as she walked. Around her wrist Jake noticed a thin, red bracelet. At first he thought it was braided metal or shiny thread, but the closer he got, the more it looked like polished stone.

Elise stopped in front of Jake and turned around. He was just able to catch himself from running into her.

"Whoa, sorry." He caught his balance and stepped back.

The Baroness look-alike narrowed her eyes yet again and sighed with annoyance.

"Are you okay, Mr. Bowman?"

"Me? Oh yeah, I'm fine. I'm just . . . taking it all in."

"I suggest you *take it in* to the locker room and put your cold weather gear on."

She pointed to a scratched-up, faded red door to the side of her. A small, rectangular sign to the left of it softly declared it was the "men's locker room."

"Then I'll show you where you'll be working."

Jake stared at the door for a moment and snuck another glance at the woman's wrists before looking back at the door.

"Mr. Bowman." Elise noticed his inadvertent hesitancy. "Are you sure you're all right?"

"Yeah. I mean, yes, I'm fine. I'll be right back."

Jake stepped past the woman, placed his hand on the scuffed steel plate affixed to the door, and pushed it open.

"Mr. Bowman," Elise's voice came from behind him, "you do know we conduct random drug tests at this facility?"

Jake balked, but only for a second before turning with a sheepish grin on his face, attempting to show his surprise at her asking *him* this question.

"Of course I do," he lied, hoping she didn't notice the color drain from his face. "I studied up before I came here this morning."

He regretted his attempt at humor. Elise didn't respond, but he knew she'd heard him. His stomach sank as he stepped into the locker room. So far, his first day was going nothing like he'd hoped.

7

THE LOCKER ROOM WAS EMPTY, but even if it were full of fellow employees, he would have plenty of room to operate comfortably without them being on top of one another. It felt odd being the only person in the locker room.

A clock hanging over a bank of mirrors next to the far row of lockers read 8:43 a.m. He couldn't believe it was already that late. He'd not been paying close attention during the training video. Even then, it hadn't seemed like that long of a film. He must have been really zoned out. Now he worried he'd missed more than he thought.

He should have asked at least one question about what he was supposed to have learned or, better yet, asked to watch it all over again, but that ship had sailed. He hoped there were very specific instructions laid out for whatever his assigned job would be. He was confident he'd be able to figure out the nuances of what he was supposed to be doing after a few days.

After a week or so, he would have it down and could then revert to his old routine of running on autopilot while staying thoroughly stoned throughout the day. Or could he? Elise had made the comment about random drug tests. He pulled the collar of his shirt up to his nose and inhaled deeply. He smelled only a mixture of cheap detergent and deodorant.

He hadn't smoked on the way to work that morning, but the scent could've attached itself to him another way. Jake's car and apartment perpetually smelled of weed, and it was quite possible the aroma had become a part of his natural musk. He was so used to the smell, it made sense Elise would be able to detect even a faint hint of pot smoke lingering while he was oblivious to it.

Maybe she didn't smell anything and had made the comment based on the impression Jake had given her. It was possible she herself was a fellow stoner and had been issuing a surreptitious warning although that seemed unlikely. He also momentarily considered neither of these scenarios was true, and he was just reading into something that wasn't there. She could have very well been reciting a piece of information to him with no pretense whatsoever. Jake was making himself extra-paranoid, and he wasn't even the least bit high.

He put it out of his mind and looked down a row of lockers, wondering how he would know which was his until he saw it at the end of the row. There was a piece of duct tape stuck to the front with "J. Bowman" written across it in black marker. A small metal plate screwed in to the locker above the tape read 312.

His name was written in a neat, feminine looking script he assumed Elise had penned. He briefly wondered if she'd written on the tape and sent a male employee in to attach it, or if she'd entered the men's locker room to do it herself. Was coming into the men's locker room something she did often and, if so, would she have no qualms with bursting in to tell him to hurry up?

He opened his locker and began to change as he indulged the thought a bit further. What if his pants were down around his ankles when she entered and—

Jake felt the smallest amount of blood beginning to pre-plump his penis from flaccid to what he referred to as a "half-chub," and he pushed the thought from his mind immediately. He was going to have a hard enough time adjusting as it was, and having locker room fantasies involving a coworker would only serve to distract him further.

Inside the bottom of Jake's locker was a combination lock with a lime-green note stuck to the back. There were numbers on the paper, quite obviously written by the same hand that labeled his locker. The numbers were *15-33-24*. The combination. He committed it to memory but shoved the paper into his back pocket just in case. Maybe if he took the note out in front of Elise, he could pretend to need help deciphering one of the numbers. It could help open a dialogue between them, and he'd know for sure whether or not she wrote it.

Again, Jake caught himself before he took the thought any further, took the note from his pocket, crumpled it, and tossed it into the bottom of his locker. He put on one of his hoodies and opted to leave the zip-up one in his locker until he experienced the cold to know if he would need it or not. He shut and secured the locker using the provided lock.

Against the wall opposite the door stretched a long rack where crisp, white lab coats hung lightly swaying in the draft from a nearby vent. Jake walked over and rooted through coats until he found a size large and pulled it on over his hoodie as he crossed to exit the locker room.

He reached for the handle to open the door and noticed the inside cuff of his lab coat was lined in red. He stepped through the door and inspected the other cuff to find the same red lining.

"If you plan on regularly taking that long in the locker room, you'll need to adjust your arrival time to compensate."

"Long? I didn't think I wa—"

"Follow me, Mr. Bowman."

Jake wanted to finish his thought, but Elise had turned around and was briskly walking down the hall he thought they came down earlier. He stepped quickly until he caught up and decided to speak as little as possible for the rest of the day.

8

JAKE CALLED MAX AND PARIS'S apartment from a pay-phone at the facility before he left for the day. No one answered. He let it ring twenty plus times before giving up and heading out to his car. Under any other circumstances, he would have waited around for a while and tried to call again, but he didn't want to spend any more time than he needed to at work.

He'd stashed a joint in the console of his car so he could "cele-brate" his first day at the main Fam-Mark facility on his drive home. After the day he'd had, he now viewed it more as a coping mecha-nism. He was going to wait until he got to the end of the street to light up, but he barely made it out of the parking lot before drawing his first puff.

By mid-day he'd already decided to ignore Elise's comment about random drug testing and throw caution to the wind. He didn't want to lose his job without having something else lined up, but giving up smoking was not going to be an option if he was going to work at this facility.

Since he hadn't smoked all day, Jake was already feeling the warm and mellow vibrations he knew so well. He'd originally planned to go home first to call Max again and check in on him but, halfway through the joint he changed his mind, deciding to stop there on his way. He was already on the route that would take him directly past Max and Paris's apartment.

No one had answered when he'd called, but he hoped it was be-cause they had gone out to grab something from the pharmacy, or maybe Max was on the mend and had gone out to grab something to eat after he'd so thoroughly emptied his body. Either way, it didn't make sense for him to go home first to call. Besides, he figured knocking on a door no one answered was more or less the same as an ever-ringing telephone. They both indicated the person or persons you were trying to reach were indeed absent.

Parking was tricky at the building where Max and his sister lived. It was hard to tell which spots were reserved and which were for visitors, but after being towed one time, Jake didn't take any chances. Since then he'd always parked a block away on the street and walked up. Today was no different. Jake sat in the Civic for ten minutes after he'd arrived to finish smoking the joint and reflect on what an odd and awful day he'd had.

Worst of all, he didn't even have Max to share in the misery, which would at least make it bearable. Actually, if what he'd experienced that first day was a taste of what was to come, Jake wasn't sure if *anything* would make it bearable. As he wandered up the sidewalk to Max's building, he started thinking about other jobs he could apply for, most of which would require he take a drug test.

He'd have to quit smoking pot immediately, then wait at least two and half weeks before applying for a position. Even then, there was no guarantee. There were other jobs he could most likely get relatively quickly, but they didn't pay anywhere close to what he would need to make his monthly nut. Suddenly Jake remembered Max might not have a job at all anymore and could be forced to take something sooner rather than later even if it meant less pay. At least he and Paris spilt the rent and bills, and Jake was sure Max's sister would kick in more than her share until he found something better.

He stood in front of apartment 213 and sighed, which turned into a cough that rattled fresh resin from his lungs. He figured his signature stoner cough could be heard through the door, and Max would open it any second to tell him to come in so he could get as stoned as Jake was. No one opened the door though.

Jake knocked three times, waited seven seconds, and knocked again harder. He stepped back and ran his hand through his hair while staring at the door, willing it to open. He stepped back quickly like he was trying to surprise the door into opening and knocked again. Actually, he didn't knock so much as he pounded seven, eight, nine times in the same way the police did half a second before they break the door down.

When no one answered after the barrage of pounding, Jake concluded the apartment was empty. He still stood at the door for two or three more minutes, trying to decide what to do next. He contemplated waiting until Max and/or Paris came back but didn't want their neighbors to complain about a stoned-looking, creepy guy skulking around their hallway. Banging as hard as he did had already, no doubt, caught some people's attention, and he imagined being watched by a single eye through the peephole of each door all the way down the hall.

He shoved his hands in his pockets and crept quickly down the hall, keeping his eyes on the floor until he got back outside. He thought about sitting in his car to wait but was already hungry when he left work and being high was starting to intensify his appetite's demand.

Jake briefly flashed to his lunch break earlier in the day, recalling how uncomfortable he'd been. He hadn't brought his lunchbox or lunch-beers, having wanted to acclimate to the vibe of the new place first, but now he wasn't sure that would ever be possible.

The vibe within the Fam-Mark facility was one he wanted nothing to do with, let alone acclimate to. Buried within the maze of hallways connecting all parts of the massive facility was an employee cafeteria. It consisted of a small counter at the far end with a kitchen behind it where you could order one of the few food choices being prepared that day. There were six long community tables with seating attached that folded up down the middle just like the ones he remembered from high school. The entire room, including the tables, was washed in a dull, off-white color from the walls down to the dingy floor tiles.

Jake had walked with his head down, trying not to be noticed by any of the employees who were at the tables eating. At his old facility everyone went on break at the same time, but here the lunches were staggered by shift due to volume of employees. The only bit of color in the cafeteria was a six-inch red stripe toward the top of the wall that ran around the entire room and disappeared into one side of the door leading into the kitchen and back out the other side, making it appear to be unbroken.

Jake had moved close enough to the counter to read the posted menu but stayed back far enough so he wouldn't be asked if he needed help. A cafeteria worker had came out from the kitchen and Jake caught a glimpse inside before the door swung back into place.

The red stripe did in fact line the walls of the kitchen.

The offerings of the day were cheese pizza, steak-fingers, or Caesar salad. Reading the menu, Jake felt like he was in high school again and wondered if it was actually the same as the food he'd eaten back then. The majority of people occupying the tables had eaten from brown bags or generic-looking, canvas totes specially lined to keep food cool. Only two people were eating what resembled one of the offerings from the menu.

Beneath the menu had been instructions stating an employee number would be needed to order food and the cost would be deducted from your check. Jake didn't know if he had an employee number or how to find out what it was. It didn't matter. He wasn't hungry anyway.

Normally he would have gone to get something to eat or just sit in his car but, as ridiculous as it sounded, he got the feeling you weren't supposed to leave the facility during breaks. His ice-cold orientation leader, Elise, hadn't specifically said as much to him, but when she told him his lunch was to be spent in the cafeteria, her tone indicated it was his only option.

Now, when Jake got back to the car his stomach shrieked like a cat in heat. He was approaching the point of being nauseous from hunger and swallowed back the bile creeping into the back of his throat. He started the car, checked his mirror, and sped away from the curb, heading for the familiar favorites he had to choose from closer to his apartment.

Once he had a full stomach, a couple of beers, and a few bong hits, he'd be able to process his day in a way that would show him it wasn't *so* bad. Maybe he'd even realize he had no reason to be paranoid and downright creeped the fuck out at all and everything would suddenly make sense. The idea eased a sliver of the despair, but Jake knew he was only paying himself lip service.

His gut cramped like it had folded in half trying to devour itself, and Jake swallowed hard again, hoping to dissuade his body from self-destructing for a few more minutes as he made the left onto his block.

9

JAKE LET THE PHONE FALL to the cradle, sending a chunk of broken plastic from the bottom flying across the room. The receiver bounced off the clear novelty base and rolled off the side of the table where it dangled and swayed inches from the ground. He'd stopped counting how many times he called Max and was now drinking himself out of driving shape earlier in the evening than usual.

He left the phone off the hook and crossed over to the window where he'd left his beer and a half-eaten piece of pizza sitting on the sill. Next to them was an ashtray with a partially smoked joint slowly dying atop a graveyard of ash-covered roaches. Jake picked up the joint first and pulled deeply to bring it back to life. The cherry on the end glowed fiery red as he perched it on the edge of the ashtray again.

The pizza was the second meal he'd had since being home, the first coming from Carson's Deli down the block. Jake liked Carson's and, while normally not his first choice, his extreme hunger dictated otherwise. Along with the turkey sub and bag of barbeque chips he was able to buy a twelve-pack of beer, which was a major advantage of having gone to the deli.

Jake inhaled half the sandwich as soon as he got into his car and finished the other half on the short drive to his apartment. By the time he walked through his door he was pouring chips into his mouth from the bag with one hand while holding an already open beer in the other. It was the second one since he'd arrived home with the first having been gulped down before he reached the stairs.

Chugging the first two beers was a mistake. Even with the sandwich and three-quarters of a bag of chips in his stomach, it was too much too fast. A warm, tingly beer-buzz snaked around his spine and massaged false confidence into his brain. The warmth glowed hotter and he felt his face go flush and mouth go dry the moment he realized he'd flown too close to the sun.

His legs were already responding to his body's distress signals and worked to move Jake in the direction of the bathroom. His feet were inches from the tile when cold, foamy beer erupted from his throat peppered with chunks of undigested sandwich. The bag of chips was still in his hand and Jake aimed the geyser of sick down into the opening. It filled up quick, but he was at the toilet by that time and finished into the bowl.

He held the bag of vomit in the palm of his hand and could feel semi-solid food pieces gently bounce around off the sides, mimicking the sensation of goldfish in a plastic sack. Jake dumped its contents in the toilet with the rest of his puke and flushed his hastily eaten meal down the commode.

The thought of it being the fastest he'd ever turned over a meal in his life would have been mildly amusing if he wasn't instantly hungry again. Usually throwing up made Jake feel better, but the pleasure was short lived as hunger clawed up the walls of his stomach, furious at having been cheated out of its offering.

He had some snacks to tide him over until the pizza arrived, and he slowly sipped at a beer while waiting. When it arrived, Jake took his time eating the first piece, chewing each bite fully, and swallowing before taking another. Halfway through the second piece he picked up his pace some, and by the third slice he was gobbling hungrily, like a starving hyena tearing quick bites of flesh from a fresh kill.

Jake felt the food producing the enzymes his system needed to level out again and he slowly began to feel like himself. He was almost full and paused after inhaling the third piece. That was when he'd started calling Max. It had been just over an hour since he'd banged on his friend's door so, when there was no answer, he wasn't overly worried.

He moved one of the only two chairs in the apartment over to the window but not before placing a cold beer next to the freshly rolled joint he'd left on the sill. Jake sat and watched the sun finish slipping below the horizon just beyond where the facility was located. As the day's light retreated, the pink glow became visible against the darkening sky.

Jake lit the joint and took a long, slow pull, filling his lungs to capacity with the thick, caramel-y smoke. He rested it on the sill to smolder and exhaled slowly through his nostrils like a lazy dragon. With the smoke fully evacuated, he brought the beer to his lips, hesitated, and put it back down again.

The last of the sunlight had been choked away beneath the dark and heavy curtain of night and, while the buildings lit up one by one on the other side of the river, the pale, pink glow was all Jake could focus on.

10

ELISE DID NOT ESCORT JAKE to where he would be actually working, but instead took him to his supervisor. Jake was glad to be rid of Elise, at least for the time being. While her Baroness-like good looks gave him a nostalgia boner, he got the impression she would like for him to be as far away from her as possible. He was unsure what he'd done to leave such a negative impression but, at least if they weren't working together, it was likely he could end up never seeing her again.

As different as this facility was, his new supervisor's office was surprisingly similar to Rob's. The room was small and stuffy with a sweet, musky scent Jake couldn't put his finger on.

The main difference between the two offices was his new supervisor, whose name was Tim, had a proper desk rather than a salvaged café table. Instead of milk crates full of papers, the back wall was lined with gray file cabinets like stoic, stone sentries standing guard over their king.

Jake sat in the chair opposite the man, waiting while he finished a phone call. At one point, Tim lowered his voice and spun his chair to face away from Jake, which reminded him of his final visit to Rob's office the day before. He still couldn't believe his old supervisor hadn't been transferred, especially since he was such a kiss-ass.

Now it made sense to Jake why Rob had been sweating more than usual, and why he was being so cryptic and secretive while on the phone. The poor guy was probably wrecked with anxiety waiting to hear if he still had a job or not. Jake was glad he hadn't been around when Rob got *that* phone call.

Tim used the hand not holding the receiver to gesticulate along with whatever he was saying, which Jake imagined had a much better effect in person. Dangling from the man's wrist was a red bracelet similar to what Elise wore, only this one was made from a braided, red cord with several knots tied into a single, dangling, short strand.

It shook violently the more expressive Tim was with the hand, making it impossible for Jake to count the knots or see any other real detail. He looked down at his hands in his lap and pulled back one of his sleeves to examine the red lining inside the cuff. He was starting to think the bracelets had something to do with a bullshit team-building activity he'd be forced to participate in sooner rather than later.

"Sorry about that."

Startled from his theorizing, Jake looked up to see Tim had finished his phone call and was turned back around in his chair. He hadn't noticed Jake's daydreaming because his eyes were looking down at the papers on his desk, which he shuffled until finding what he was looking for.

"So, Jacob, is it?" Tim continued while still looking at the selected piece of paper. "Or do you go by Jake?"

"Oh, I go by Jake." He extended his hand across the desk to formally meet his new supervisor.

Tim kept his eyes down on the paper and didn't notice, letting the gesture hang awkwardly unrequited. Jake slowly withdrew his hand, trying to play it off as if he were stretching, and adjusted himself in the chair. He noticed Tim wore a red bracelet around his other wrist as well, but the knotted thread hanging from it was considerably shorter than the other. Jake cringed internally as he momentarily revisited the idea of having to not only participate in a team-building activity, but also being made to wear ridiculous bracelets to show he was "on board."

While the office was similar to Rob's, the man who occupied it was not. Tim was poised, confident, and deliberate with his movements. Even the way he talked with his hand while on the phone served some purpose Jake was simply not aware of. His shirt was crisp and not wilted by sweat from under his arms or around the collar.

His tie was tight and straight and, at first glance, appeared completely black, but after stealing another look, Jake saw a thin red line running down the center. He would have missed it completely had the light not been at just the right angle. Otherwise, it was a minute detail easy to miss.

"I see you're amongst those transferred over from the now de-funct 'health and wellness line' facility. You're lucky."

Jake balked for a moment, trying to imagine what Tim's defini-tion of "lucky" was, but he was more interested in what Tim said about him being amongst those transferred over. He said *those*, im-plying there was at least more than one person who transferred. Elise had either been mistaken or possibly even hazing him. He didn't care now. This meant there was still a possibility Jake would be working alongside Max again.

"Do you happen to know who the others are?" Jake blurted the question quickly and with no context attached.

"What was that?"

Tim was still holding the paper between his fingers, but had now looked up at Jake for the first time. Realizing his misstep, Jake reeled in his eagerness before starting again.

"I'm sorry," he began. "I meant to ask if you happened to know who else was transferred in from my old facility?"

Tim crinkled his features into an annoyed expression suggesting Jake's question was a waste of his time.

"No," he said flatly, turning his attention back down to the pa-per in his hand. "No, I do not."

"I was just curious." Jake continued, well aware he was pushing his luck. "Elise told me I was the only one, but she must have been mistaken."

Tim glanced up and, for a moment, his eyes met Jake's before darting back to the page. Tim would be answering no more ques-tions regarding the matter.

"Since you have experience, the transition shouldn't be a prob-lem for you, I presume."

Jake didn't know if Tim was asking or telling him, so he kept his mouth shut but nodded a non-verbal response just in case. Beads of sweat perched at the edge of his pores in their infancy stage, trying to decide if they should come out or not, reminding Jake of his old supervisor. He wore layers and a lab coat, but the stifling and overall uncomfortable vibe of the office was what pulled the perspiration from Jake's face. He was starting to think they were giving him a little too much credit. He suddenly very much regretted not paying attention to the video Elise showed him.

"Of course," Tim continued, looking up from the paper again, "we'll start you off slow before we put you on any of *these* machines."

The condescending way Tim said the word *these* would have bothered Jake under different circumstances. He loathed being talked down to in any way, but now he hardly noticed.

"We're still figuring out where to put some people, so your first week or so you'll be shuffled around doing non-machine related work. Once things get settled, you'll be assigned your permanent position."

If Jake weren't so out of sorts and distracted by this new environment, he might have picked up on the unsettling way Tim said *permanent*. It wasn't condescending or patronizing this time but was as unsettling as it was foreboding. He also didn't notice Tim's mouth curve upward ever so slightly when he finished the sentence.

The way Tim talked about "figuring out where to put people" and "once things get settled" made it sound like there were, for sure, more new people than just Jake coming into the mix. Momentarily lost in the rush of excitement, he didn't notice Tim stand up and look down with a scowl.

"I said, follow me."

"Sorry, sir." Jake stumbled up and out of the chair.

His use of the word "sir" surprised him, since he would never have thought to call Rob sir. Something about the way his new supervisor conducted himself seemed to demand the verbal sign of respect.

"For the rest of the day you'll be in The Box," Tim said after a short huff of a sigh. "You did work in The Box at your last facility, yes?"

"Yes." Jake tried to keep his tone from betraying how he felt. "Yes, sir, I sure did."

Tim said nothing as he walked around the desk and out of the small office. Jake fell directly in line behind him, dreading the task his supervisor laid before him. He had worked in The Box at the other facility, but it was a task he would do anything to avoid. He'd paid other employees several times to switch jobs with him for the day while others were placated into doing it with a joint or two.

The production rooms were cold but, compared to The Box, they may as well have been steam-filled saunas. While the product was produced in a cold setting, it was stored in an even colder one. Jake was able to tolerate the forty-degree temperature of the production room, although it took a while and several different combinations of layers before he was somewhat comfortable.

The Box was another story altogether. The temperature within was at negative twenty degrees Fahrenheit in order to prepare the ice cream for shipping. Refrigerated trucks could safely transport the product but, since it wasn't a completely controlled environment, the temperature was subject to fluctuate. This was why all product was stored in The Box for twenty-four hours before being shipped out. The extreme cold ensured it would reach its destination unspoiled.

If you were assigned to The Box for the day, it was your job to organize flavors on wooden pallets for shipping according to the order and where it was being sent. Working The Box required you wear a special, thickly lined jumpsuit, and every hour you had to step outside for thirty minutes to avoid frostbite and hypothermia. It was a miserable and laborious task that dragged on and on, especially since you were forced to watch each second of the day more or less tick away in a torturous fashion.

Jake followed Tim down the hall, plunging impossibly deeper into the center of the mammoth facility. The different hallways disoriented Jake. He was unable to tell which direction they went or what side of the building they were on. All the changing of direction made the hallways feel like they were too long to be contained within the building.

Having entered through the front, Jake had no idea how far back the facility went. It was possible the building extended back onto the property behind it, but it was difficult to spatially visualize something so big.

Several summers ago, Jake had seen a cruise ship docked from the window of a beach house he and some friends had rented for the weekend. Up close, it had been huge, resembling a skyscraper lying on its side. Seeing something so big made Jake feel small and powerless, exactly how the facility made him feel now.

After walking through the seemingly endless hallways for far longer than should have been possible, Tim finally stopped. Jake knew the door they stood in front of led to The Box. It was similar to the one from the other facility. The diamond-cut kick plate running across the lower half of the door was a dead giveaway.

Jake noticed the same red line running down each side of the wall, still seemingly unbroken. He tried not to think about it.

"I know it seems confusing now, but it won't take long for you to become familiar with the layout of the facility."

Jake chose to believe the statement was something Tim said to all new people while showing them around and not because the supervisor could be reading his mind. He nodded his response, not wanting to speak unless it was absolutely necessary. His quips hadn't gone over well with Elise, and Jake didn't want to come off as a wise-ass to his new boss.

Tim turned to the door, grabbed the silver latch on the right, and pulled down. An extended hiss sounded as the seal relinquished its hold from the metal frame with exaggerated reluctance. It opened to a staging area far more elaborate than Jake was used to. Across the room, directly in front of them, was the door leading into the actual Box. To the right of it was a pane of three-inch thick glass, a safety window embedded in the wall.

The window was four feet by three feet and allowed for someone to watch the person in The Box in case something happened. The two were supposed to switch out every thirty minutes, to take the required break every hour.

On the wall to their right, two specially lined, thermal jumpsuits dangled from hooks. Clipboards and a poster warning against the dangers of extreme cold hung to the left. Another poster hung beside it with first-aid instructions on what to do in case of hypothermia or frostbite, as well as how to properly administer CPR.

Jake wandered over to the window and saw The Box was much bigger at this facility, meaning more work, naturally. There was one difference he noticed right away though; there was no load-out door built into the back wall of The Box. Without one, how was the forklift supposed to load the pallets from The Box to the truck?

He figured he was just missing it but, if so, he was unable to tell what could be obscuring its location. He was about to ask about it, but Tim spoke first.

"Take it off," he said.

"What was that?" Jake was sure he'd misheard his supervisor. It sounded like something you'd hear shouted at a strip club.

"Take off your clothes."

Jake paused, confused, and suddenly wondered where the other part of the two-person team it took to work The Box was. He couldn't do it by himself, and there were two suits after all. He looked over at the jumpsuits again and noticed something different about the staging room.

There was no red stripe along the wall.

He'd noticed the stripe ran along the halls since he entered the facility, continuing unbroken, plunging around doorframes to circle each room before exiting the other side of the frame where it continued on its way. A quick glance back through the thick window showed the red line was absent from The Box as well as the staging room.

"So," Jake again pointed to the jumpsuits, "you mean I have to go back down to the locker room and change or—"

"No," Tim interrupted. "I *mean* take your clothes off here. Now."

"Is that a new thing, because we ne—"

"Now!"

The authoritative halt with which the supervisor delivered his command was jarring in the small and otherwise quiet room. The tiny amount of echo decayed quickly, making it sound like a touch of reverb had been added to Tim's voice. The effect made his demand sound more terrifying and forceful.

Jake wasn't sure what he was going to do, or if his new supervisor was truly serious, but he started to unbutton his lab coat while quickly running through options in his head. He could probably make a break for it and get past Tim fairly easily. Jake really wished he'd paid more attention to the video. Maybe he'd missed some vital information that could possibly make sense of this.

Was he really supposed to take all his clothes off in this room right in front of his new supervisor? *Could* he even do that? The thought of him standing naked in front of Tim was confusing in itself, but the miniscule amount of excitement he felt didn't help either.

From there his mind went back to thoughts of Elise in the locker room, only this time she stepped into the room with Tim, wearing nothing but a lab coat one size too small. Jake stepped over to the wall and hung his lab coat on a hook next to one of the jumpsuits.

He imagined Tim turning around to open Elise's coat slowly, one button at a time. Lost in the fantasy again, Jake didn't realize he'd started taking his shirt off until Tim barked again, snapping him back to reality.

"Mr. Bowman, what are you doing?"

Jake froze with his shirt pulled up to his chest and his stomach exposed, wondering the same thing. He let his shirt fall back into place while chewing on the words he was attempting to say, succeeding only in breaking apart syllables that leapt one at a time from his stuttering lips.

"I—I—I thought . . ."

Jake was completely thrown by how sudden and invasive his fantasy was, as if he had no control over it. He'd had his fair share of daydreams back at the old facility when he was bored, but those were organic and wholly his own. He felt as if this scenario was beamed into his head by force, like when the news breaks during your regularly scheduled programming to announce the latest tragedy.

"I thought you said to take off my . . . clothes?" Jake finally managed to answer the supervisor.

"Coat!" Tim said, enunciating loudly. "I said take off your *coat.* You don't need it with the jumpsuit on."

Coat? *Coat?* Jake was sure he'd heard "clothes," hadn't he? But then again, why would Tim tell him to take off his clothes? There was a soft rumble from the fans keeping the staging area cold and The Box colder, so it was possible the sound prevented him from hearing correctly. This was the foundation for a rationalization Jake would continue to formulate in his head for the rest of the day.

"Take your *clothes* off?" Tim chuckled, the only sign of emotion he'd shown since Jake had been with him. "Mr. Bowman, I don't know how you did things at the *other* facility, but we like to keep our clothes on here while working."

Jake didn't know how to respond so he went back into silent mode, choosing to smile and nod in lieu of verbal response. He reached for the jumpsuit and stepped into it one leg at a time before pulling it up over his body to slip his arms through the designated holes. Tim had laughed at the mix-up, but Jake couldn't gauge if it was lighthearted or judgmental.

"Oh, Mr. Bowman," the supervisor started, his tone now void of whimsy, "Elise did mention our random drug test policy, didn't she?"

11

WHEN HIS ALARM WENT OFF Jake immediately regretted drinking the night before. The pressure behind his eyes was so intense he wouldn't have been surprised if they burst to allow the physical manifestation of his pain to escape in the form of a large, spike-covered worm. His mouth was bone-dry with a deeply offensive sour taste baked into his tongue by heat from the bile slowly creeping up his throat.

Jake smacked his lips, hoping to coax even the tiniest bit of moisture back into his mouth but succeeded only in making himself nauseous. He swung his legs off the side of his bed, intending to stand up, but stumbled forward, falling to one knee instead. He steadied himself with his hands against the floor to keep from tumbling forward and quickly popped to his feet and raced to the toilet.

Two minutes later he was flushing his second meal in the last twelve hours down the toilet, leaving him weak and empty inside. He sat on the closed toilet lid rubbing his palms into his eyes to massage away his headache like he'd seen hung-over people in movies do. It did nothing to alleviate the pain. He sighed, forced himself to stand, and shuffled two feet to his right on shaky legs, gripping the sink to keep balanced.

He turned the faucet on, put his mouth beneath it, and lapped at the steady stream like a dying beast arriving at an oasis, hoping to drink the life back into itself. Then he remembered Max. The thought provided a temporary rejuvenation, allowing him to run to the phone without falling over.

The receiver still dangled off the side of his nightstand from the cracked plastic base. The memory of dropping the phone on the final attempt to reach his friend the night before flashed in his mind like an out-of-focus polaroid. The phone was off the hook all night. Jake bit back another wave of nausea as he bent to snatch it up.

He expected to put the receiver to his ear and hear the continuous, shrill, bleating sound alerting him he hadn't hung up his phone properly, but there was nothing. He pressed the button on the base to summon a dial tone but it would not come despite trying several times.

Frustrated, he grabbed the phone's base to make sure the cord was plugged in and saw right away what the problem was. He must have dropped the receiver onto the base a lot harder than he thought because, not only had a chunk broken off, but the once clearish plastic was marred with cracks. They shot off from the point of impact in all directions like ancient spiderwebs preserved in ice.

Something within the base rattled and, while the cracks prohibited him from seeing exactly what had broken inside, it didn't matter because, either way, the phone was still done. It wasn't like he could solder some random pieces together and it would all of a sudden work. The phone was now trash.

The clock next to the now empty spot where the phone had been told Jake he'd have to hustle to get to work on time. He briefly contemplated stopping by Max's on the way to bang on the door one more time, but he was already running late as it was. He decided to call from the facility as soon as he had a chance.

He couldn't remember if there was a payphone in the men's locker room but, if not, he might have to wait until his lunch break to try and call. He rushed through a shower while brushing his teeth feverishly, trying to banish the scent of beer and vomit from his breath. He got dressed and put on his shoes, briefly thinking about his first day, and felt nauseous all over again but for a completely different reason.

12

JAKE SHIVERED JUST THINKING ABOUT being in The Box as he begrudgingly headed to the new facility for his second day. It turned out he actually did have to work in The Box alone for the rest of the day, which Tim flippantly explained with the same line he gave Jake earlier about shuffling around people and positions.

Jake had glanced across the room the day before at a sign next to the safety posters that said: *A Minimum Of Two People Must Be Working This Station At ALL Times.* He'd thought Tim might follow his eyes, see the sign, and suddenly remember another person needed to be there, but when Jake looked back, Tim was turning to leave.

"What needs to be done first is on the clipboard with the rest listed in order of priority." Tim pushed the door open, coaxing another hiss from the reluctant safety seal, paused, and turned around to face Jake again. "Welcome aboard, Mr. Bowman," he'd said.

Welcome aboard.

The words held the gravitas of a death sentence and fell from Tim's mouth like grand pianos being pushed off the Empire State Building, voiding the statement of the intended sentiment.

Welcome aboard.

Now Jake turned up the radio in his car to distract him from thinking about it anymore. Miraculously, he'd hit all green lights on his way in and made up enough time to not be late. There wouldn't be time for him to call Max before work; he'd have to do it at lunch.

He wasn't looking forward to working in The Box again all day and hoped there would be another person with him to help shoulder the load. Jake had been joined briefly the afternoon prior but, at the end of the day, after all the pallets had been assembled. A man named Ian or Ivan, Jake didn't pay close attention, came in to show him how to arrange the pallets so they could be loaded onto the truck.

Jake still hadn't seen the seam of a load out door in the frigid room, but he was too tired and hungry by then to care. Ian/Ivan had Jake arrange the pallets toward the center of the freezing room offset from each other with six-inch gaps in-between. The arrangement had seemed frantic to Jake and didn't make any sense but, so far, a lot of things about the facility hadn't made sense. When he'd finished with the placement of the product, he'd came back in the staging room to find it empty.

If Jake had to work with Ian/Ivan it would be better than nothing but not by much. There was something about him Jake didn't like, but he couldn't put his finger on it exactly. The man had been curt when he spoke but Jake took no offense, and nothing out of the ordinary was said.

Jake figured Ian/Ivan was in as big a hurry to leave as he was, so he hadn't thought twice when he'd noticed the man shifting his weight back and forth between his feet. What if Ian/Ivan was in a hurry not because he'd wanted to go home, but because he'd wanted to be out of that room and away from The Box? The man's behavior gave Jake the impression The Box was equally disliked, but for entirely different reasons than he and his old coworkers had.

Now Jake walked through the front doors of the facility exactly on time, paused for a second to get his bearings, and headed in what he thought was the direction of the locker room. There were actually other people in the hall this morning, and Jake wondered if he would even recognize Ian/Ivan if he walked by or ran into him in the locker room.

His eyes wandered up the wall as he walked and fixed absently on the never-ending red line running up and down both sides. He zoned out and, in his mind, saw an image of himself walking a narrow, red road lined on both sides with people wearing white Fam-Mark lab coats.

Something about their facial features was so intrinsically simple they almost didn't exist. The faces were similar, different enough to not be exactly alike, and yet instantly forgettable at the same time. Jake thought of Ian/Ivan in the same way. The man was clearly somebody, an actual person, but as far as Jake could recall, he may as well not even had a face.

The red road looked like it went on forever, but off in the far distance Jake could see the pink glow radiating from a raging inferno with flames the same color. He felt the heat intensify with each step and thought he heard screams coming from the blaze, but he couldn't stop. Something was compelling him to keep going. Something was driving him.

Jake was ripped from his mid-morning daydream when he suddenly collided with the person in front of him. He was so deep in his own thoughts he didn't realize someone had stopped and turned around to talk to him. It was Elise.

For a petite woman, she was incredibly strong and solid. Jake wasn't moving fast, but he did run into her without slowing down and she didn't budge an inch. Jake, on the other hand, tripped on his own foot and stumbled backward, dropping his hoodie and lunchbox as he reached to steady himself against the wall.

The latch on the metal, horror-themed lunchbox popped open when it hit the faux-dingy tile and three pieces of last night's pizza flopped out onto the floor. Not wanting to go hungry again, he'd thrown them in the lunchbox in haste as he was leaving the apartment without bothering to put them in a plastic bag or wrap them in cellophane. In fact, Jake was sure he didn't have either of those things.

He froze, staring at the individual pieces of pizza lying cold and limp in sharp contrast against the tile like long dead fish left out on the dock by lazy fishermen who couldn't be bothered with throwing them back. He looked up at Elise, now realizing what had happened, and launched into apology mode.

"Oh, man, I'm so sorry." He bent over to scoop the ruined slices back into the box. The act itself was almost as embarrassing as running into her, but having to push ruined pizza into a children's lunchbox added a touch of sadness to the whole experience.

Elise watched him fumble with his ruined lunch while hugging her trusty clipboard to her chest without comment. Jake started to stand up, but dropped back down to pick up his hoodie that ended up behind him somehow.

"I'm really sorry about that, Elise," Jake said again upon standing. "Are you okay? I wasn't paying attention, and I—"

"You were daydreaming again," she said.

Again? She said it like she knew Jake had a propensity to daydream after having only spent a handful of minutes with him. He hoped he hadn't appeared so obviously distracted the day before but, the way Elise said it, the careful enunciation of the word "daydream" told him he had done just that.

"Well, yeah, actually I . . . was."

Jake was caught daydreaming by Rob plenty of times at the other facility, and he wondered if the supervisor secretly kept track in some permanent employee file Elise studied before he'd arrived. He never cared for his old boss but, for a moment, he missed the sweaty old asshole. Rob may have been an uptight hard-ass but, right now, Jake would take that over the cold oddness of the people at this facility a hundred times over.

Elise nodded and pulled the clipboard away from her chest to read something from the top of the page before clutching it to her chest again. Jake noticed the red bracelets clinging snugly to her exposed wrists. She hadn't stood like that the day prior when she'd showed him around, and Jake's stomach sunk at the realization she might be purposely covering herself because of him.

He didn't know why. He'd barely spent any time with her the day before, and they'd interacted minimally. She was so stoic, so cold, it was impossible for him to read her. Did she have the ability to look into his mind somehow? Did she know how he'd thought about her in the locker room?

"Do you know a Maxwell Clark."

It was a question but she said it more like a statement. Jake wasn't used to hearing his friend's full name said out loud, and it took him a second to realize it was *his* Max.

"Max!" he blurted excitedly. "I mean, Maxwell. Yeah. Yes, I know him. Why are you asking?"

"He was supposed to meet me at the front an hour ago for orientation, but didn't show up. According to his file he transferred in with you, so I wanted to see if you'd heard from him."

Jake couldn't believe what he was hearing. First there were no other transfers, and then there was, and now one of them was Max. He was as confused as he was excited.

"I—I thought you said I was the only transfer?"

"You were," she spat. "You were the only transfer coming in yesterday. The start dates have been staggered to ensure proper, one-on-one training."

Jake wanted to argue that she hadn't made herself clear at all and should probably learn to communicate better, especially if her job was to deal with people, but it didn't matter at the moment. Max had been transferred, and soon they would be back to their old routine.

"Oh, you know what?" Jake started. "He's been really sick. I don't think he'd be well enough to come in today."

"Sick?" Elise narrowed her eyes and peeked quickly at the clipboard again. "He didn't mention anything about being sick when I spoke with him on the phone yesterday."

13

JAKE RAN THROUGH THE PARKING lot to his car and for the first time noticed the red stripe painted on the ground as he stepped over it. He didn't wonder if it circled the entire facility because he already knew it did. Investigating would not be necessary, at least not right now.

He'd been stuck in The Box again all day, alone, and Tim only came by to check on him once. While Jake did like being left to his own devices under extremely light supervision, there was too much work for him to truly enjoy the freedom, and he wasn't familiar enough with how things worked to take advantage of the situation. Since he had no help, it took him all day to complete the pallets as they were assigned on the clipboard waiting for him when he arrived. Tim must have come in early and replaced the list from yesterday because it was gone, the current day's workload left in its place.

He was doubly frustrated when it became apparent he was going to have to work through lunch and wouldn't have a chance to call Max. He'd ended up eating two of the three slices of pizza since the third was covered in too much hair and dirt for him to ignore. The only thing keeping him from having a meltdown was knowing Max was at the facility or, at least according to Elise, he was supposed to be, and probably undergoing the same strange training he'd experienced.

Still, if Max was well enough to come to work why didn't he answer the phone? Why didn't he answer the door? If Elise spoke to him, when the hell did she do it? He thought about his phone being

51

not only off the hook, but broken. A call from Max may have come late last night or early this morning, but he wouldn't have known because he no longer had a working phone. He would have to pick one up on his way home, but his first stop would be Max's place.

Something else bothered Jake about his interaction with Elise that morning. She'd hugged the clipboard against her chest in a way that made him feel like she was doing it purposely because she didn't want her breasts to be ogled by *him* specifically. He could have been wrong, had hoped he was wrong in his reading of the situation, but he couldn't read Elise at all. During their brief exchange, after Jake shoved his floor-pizza back into his lunchbox, he made sure to look her in the eye, not allowing his gaze to drift southward in the slightest.

When she'd mentioned Max, he momentarily forgot about the whole thing until the conclusion of their conversation. When Elise told him she was going to her office to check her messages, she lowered her arms and placed her hands behind her back, which pushed her chest out slightly.

With the clipboard gone Jake couldn't help but look down at the very hard, very noticeable nipples pressing through her lab coat like torpedoes begging to be launched from a submarine. He'd been caught off guard and tried to redirect his line of sight, but the pause she took before walking away was what confused him most.

Had she done that on purpose? It was like she'd held the clipboard there to tease him before the "grand reveal," but why would she do that?

Jake tried to blame it solely on his own perverted mind subconsciously bathing the situation in a sexual light, but a small part of him still believed there was more to it. Also, he only caught a quick glimpse and couldn't be sure, but Jake swore Elise was topless beneath the lab coat.

That was just his imagination though. Women didn't walk around topless under a tight white coat unless they were at the very beginning or possibly the very, very end of a porno film. Fam-Mark was a professional business and things like that didn't happen at professional businesses, and they most certainly didn't happen to Jake.

He jumped in his car, snagged the joint he'd left in his visor, and went to light up before starting the engine. He didn't bother waiting this time. His fingers were still tingling from working in The Box all day and the pins and needles made it difficult to flick the lighter, but after three attempts he was able to coax out a flame. Jake turned the key in the ignition as he inhaled, threw the car in gear, and sped from the lot, accidently cutting off another exiting co-worker.

Half a mile down the road, cars were crawling due to a lane closure, and once he got past it, traffic was thicker than it had been the day before at the same time. The lights that were green for Jake in the morning now screamed red at every intersection. He'd been on the road for forty-five minutes and was still two blocks away from Max's apartment. Thanks to a fender-bender at the final light, it took twenty more to make it the rest of the way.

When he turned onto Max's street the curb was lined up and down with cars, leaving Jake nowhere to park. This happened sometimes but, he found, after circling the block once or twice something would open up. Most likely a lot of the cars belonged to people who'd run into the drug and/or liquor store at either corner and would be leaving soon.

Jake circled the block upward of ten times and not a single spot opened up. At first he thought he might have been losing recently opened spots to other drivers when he happened to be on the other side of the block. It didn't take long for him to figure out no one was swooping in to take newly opened spots behind him because the cars never changed. They were the same each and every time he made the block, prompting him to think there must be a gathering or party of some sort within the apartment complex.

It was the only explanation he could come up with for why the cars didn't move. He'd hung out at Max's place before for hours, leaving his car parked on the street late into the night, so it was possible the same thing was happening but on a bigger scale. With twenty more minutes behind him spent on what was turning out to be a fool's errand, he snaked through the surrounding streets until he found a space five blocks over.

The impending walk made him wish he'd brought another joint, or at least a pipe to smoke the few roaches in his ashtray. When he left his place that morning, he didn't count on his errands taking long, so he only brought the one joint with him. If he wasn't in such a hurry now, Jake would run into the liquor store at the other end of the block, but that would mean passing Max's apartment to get there.

At this point, doubling back was too much of a risk. He was on foot now but, even so, that didn't mean something couldn't happen to deter him further. He imagined running in to grab a quick tallboy of whatever was cheapest and accidently interrupting a holdup in progress. He'd end up stuck in some hostage situation all night, keeping him from getting to Max's once again but somehow being over in time for him to get to work on time in the morning.

If Max was home, Jake would snag a beer or two from his fridge before listening to his friend explain why he couldn't be reached for almost three days. He walked through the complex, keeping his eyes and ears open for the kind of noise associated with parties, but he didn't start to hear it until he approached Max's apartment.

When Jake rounded the corner, it was clear the noise was coming from one of the units on the same row as his friend, and he wondered if it was Max's neighbor to the left who was cool, or the one on the right who was a total bitch. Either way, Jake figured he could scam a few beers from one or the other before being asked to stay or leave.

He stopped within steps of Max's apartment, confused as an uncomfortably warm wave of anger started at his head and pushed cleanly down across the rest of him. The party was going on behind the door Jake was standing in front of. One day his best friend was so ill he could barely walk, and the next he's starting at the facility while also having a mega-party. Jake couldn't decide if he was more angry or hurt he hadn't been invited.

He stopped and breathed, trying to keep from reacting emotionally. As odd as the situation seemed, he knew there had to be an explanation, so he checked his anger until he had an actual reason to feel it. Normally he would have knocked but, since it was clear there was a party going on inside, he decided to walk in.

He reached for the knob but pulled his hand back just as his fingers grazed it, reacting like the metal was heated or electronically charged. Neither of those were the case, but Jake found himself wishing it had been one or the other. His heart raced, his stomach sank, and his breath hitched.

Dangling from the doorknob was a red bracelet.

14

THE DOOR OPENED BEFORE JAKE could reach out to make a second attempt.

"Hey there, Jacob! I thought I heard someone knock."

He had not knocked.

It was Tim. Jake's new boss stood in his best friend's apartment with a party going on behind him.

"I hope you don't mind my informality in using your first name," Tim continued. "It's after working hours, so let's save all that boring stuff for the office."

Tim's smile didn't sit right on his face, not like it didn't belong there, but like it wasn't *supposed* to be there. It warped the rest of his facial features, giving him an overall cartoonish quality.

It made Jake think about the time he saw his fourth-grade teacher, Mr. Morris, in the grocery store. It was the first time he'd seen a teacher outside of school, and the concept of them being actual people with actual lives was overwhelming. For whatever reason, at the time, he equated the experience to encountering one of his favorite cartoon characters hanging out in the real world. It just shouldn't be.

"Jacob? Jacob? Are you okay?"

For a moment Jake wasn't okay. Black dots crept from the sides of his eyes and worked their way across until they'd eclipsed his vision completely. He wasn't sure how long he'd been staring at the darkness before the dots broke apart again and again until they weren't there anymore.

"What? Yeah," Jake finally managed. "I didn't think . . . uh . . . I didn't . . . is there a part—"

"Of course it's a party," Tim cut him off as he stepped out of the doorframe and brought a hand down on Jake's shoulder a bit harder than he expected. "Max invited us over to celebrate his new position at the facility, but I'm sure you know all about that. Get on in here and grab yourself a drink."

Before Jake could answer, he'd been pulled past the threshold and into the apartment with the door slamming right behind him. He didn't close the door though, or did he? He must have grabbed the handle and pulled it shut behind him out of force of habit, but he was usually careful not to slam the door. Jake knew what it was like to have a neighbor in his apartment building that slammed the door all the time, and he didn't want to be *that* guy.

"Max has been telling us all about what great friends the two of you are."

When Tim spoke, his face took on a particularly off-putting quality, making it hard for Jake to look directly at.

"He has?" Jake turned his neck to look behind him. "Where is M—"

Tim's hand was still on Jake's shoulder. He moved it closer to his neck and squeezed to direct his attention back onto him.

"Oh, he's around here somewhere." Tim gestured vaguely with his free hand, a hand now holding a big, fat joint between its spindly, thin fingers. "He told me to give you this though."

Tim held the joint up in front of Jake's face close enough to smell the characteristics indicating its high potency. The joint found its way between Jake's lips through some sleight of hand on Tim's part, and it dangled for a moment before the supervisor retrieved a lighter from the pocket of his slacks and touched it with the fiery tip. Jake's eyes focused on the red bracelet snuggly hugging Tim's wrist and found himself pulling on the joint, acting on instinct alone.

"I did tell you we randomly drug test, right?"

Tim winked and slipped the lighter back into his pocket. The nauseating smile hung from his face like a portrait on a wall too small to fully accommodate, thereby adding to the level of confusion it evoked.

15

JAKE STOOD IN HIS BEST friend's apartment with people who were essentially strangers. He smoked a very powerful joint between sips from a bottle of beer that was shoved into his hand. By whom, Jake didn't see and at this point it didn't matter. He became quickly consumed by the strange reality he stumbled upon.

Elise didn't say anything to Jake when she walked up behind Tim, and acknowledged him only with the familiar scowl his presence evoked. She stepped close to Tim and whispered something in his ear as he nodded, listening intently. With the message delivered, she turned to walk away. Jake noticed she still wore her lab coat with a bright red thong showing through the tight white material.

"Excuse me, Jacob," Tim said. "I need to take care of something."

With no added elaboration, Tim turned on his heels and followed Elise down the dark hallway toward Max and Paris's bedrooms. Jake sucked hard on the joint, pretending he hadn't noticed the outline of Tim's growing erection as it struggled against the confines of his slacks.

He didn't have time to take another step before a semi-familiar face approached him. Ian/Ivan had stuck his hand out to shake Jake's but held it up a little too high. It was like he was filming a scene and the director told him to keep his hand and chest level so it stayed in frame.

"Hey, Jake, right? It's me, Ivan. I helped you in The Box yesterday."

Jake knew two things about the man for sure: his name was Ivan, and the two of them had very different definitions of "help."

57

The man talked at Jake rather than to him, but everything he said was garbled and hadn't made any sense, at least to Jake. It sounded like Ivan was starting in the middle of sentences while ending a thought in the middle of another. It was possible the combination of the gifted weed and the beer he didn't realize he'd already chugged was impairing him slightly.

Still, even with the talking and music in the background, Jake could hear well enough to know the things Ivan was saying made no sense.

One of the two beers Ivan was holding found its way into Jake's hand, being surreptitiously swapped for the empty bottle dangling by its neck from his fingertips. Jake had looked over his shoulder and scanned the room for another familiar face but didn't recognize a single person. He'd been in Max's place dozens of times and spent countless hours there but, filled with strangers, it felt completely foreign to him.

Jake muttered a half-audible "excuse me" and brushed past Ivan in mid-incoherent sentence. The man didn't seemed to mind or even notice, and Jake still heard him talking as he started down the hall.

By process of elimination Max was either in his room, Paris's room, or the bathroom, and Jake was quickly approaching all three options.

The only door open was the bathroom where two men stood outside, talking to a woman leaning up against the doorframe. The first door on his right was Paris's room, so he figured he'd check there first.

"Oh hey, I wouldn't go in there."

Jake's hand rested on the doorknob as the warning came from the woman standing by the bathroom.

"Excuse me?" He'd looked around to make sure she was indeed talking to him before continuing. "It's okay, she's a good friend of mine."

"The girl in that room is sick," the woman offered. "I mean she is *sick* sick. Her brother said he doesn't want anyone bothering her under any circumstances."

"Her brother? Do you happen to know where Max is?"

"Um . . ." The woman looked back and forth between the two men who shook their heads. "I just saw him. Maybe he's back in the living room."

Unless Max passed Jake in the hall by crawling on the ceiling like in *The Exorcist III,* he was most certainly not in the living room.

Max's door was directly across from the bathroom and Jake walked to it without making eye contact with the three bathroom lurkers.

"I wouldn't go in there eith—"

"I know what I'm doing, okay!"

Jake cut the woman off mid-warning, surprised by how quickly frustrated he became for being as stoned as he was. He just needed to get to Max.

An awkward moment floated between Jake and the woman while the two other men stepped back to keep out of the way of the potential line of fire. Jake saw past the woman into the bathroom where a small, square mirror sat next to the sink topped with a liberal amount of cocaine.

Finger smudges running through rows of white crumbs next to the pile signified the party had been going on for a while. It was only then Jake noticed the three sniffing almost in unison.

"Sorry." Jake had softly held his hands up. "But . . . uh . . . I'm supposed to be in there."

"Suit yourself." She stepped into the bathroom and leaned over the sink to carve another line from the snowbank on the mirror. "No skin off my dick."

She snorted the line through a straw she was holding in two quick bursts between the last two words of her sentence. He nodded, turned to open the door, and walked into Max's room.

The headboard of Max's bed was pushed up against the middle of the wall directly across from the door. A man lay in the bed with his head where his feet should have been. He was on his back with the naked body of Elise straddling him while viciously grinding her genitals against his groin.

Under normal circumstances, getting to see Elise naked—even accidentally—would've been a highlight to file away in his spank-bank for later use.

Her skin was taut, with light musculature showing through her arms, what he could see of her thighs, and the upper portion of her midsection below her breasts. Her stomach was flat with a subtle softness to it, a particular feature Jake always found attractive in women. Her breasts were full and natural, judging by the way they hung with an intangible curvature unable to be duplicated in the uncanny valley of fake breasts.

The nipples fighting to rip through the fabric of her lab coat earlier in the day were now free and on display. They perched at the center of each soft, white breast like tiny, light-pink bullets fitted especially for a twenty-two caliber Derringer.

Every bit of pleasantness her nude form exuded was instantly marred and forever ruined by the head resting on her petite, seductive body. Gone were the appealing facial features granted from winning several aspects of the genetic lottery, as well as the soft, straight, ultra-black hair. What existed in their place would cause the most devout person of faith to question the existence of their god.

To say it was the head of a dog would be an easy way to describe it, only this didn't look like any dog Jake had ever seen. The first and most obvious off-putting characteristic was the size of the head. It was large, too large for the body it crowned by two to three times. The general shape and distinctness of its snout reminded Jake of a pitbull, only the jowls were far more menacing than any member of the species.

Its maw hung open, revealing what looked like an impossible amount of teeth, each sharpened to a point, and even from nine feet away Jake saw their serrated edges. Running up its forehead, between its ears, and down the back of its neck protruded a row of curved, black spikes that got larger the farther back they went, like a futuristic, battle-modified Rhodesian Ridgeback.

The eyes were slick, moist, onyx orbs with no differentiation between iris and pupil. They stood out like shiny black domes amidst the short, dark hair covering the head like the ruined bristles of a chimney sweep. Its ears pointed up and back on either side of the monstrous head like antennas on a sci-fi space helmet.

The sight was so jarring Jake didn't notice the collar until last. It was made of red, braided cord like a larger version of the bracelets everyone at the facility was wearing, and attached was a matching leash running down between her breasts, ending in the grasp of Tim's clutches. Jake caught something moving out of the corner of his eye and allowed himself a quick look for fear something equally awful may be coiled to pounce.

Against the wall on the right side of the room was Max's desk. The black pleather chair, which was occupied, was turned to face the bed. Jake saw the person's pants on the floor bunched between their feet and could tell from the movement of their upper body they were furiously masturbating. He could also tell from the back of his head it was Max.

Jake backed out of the room but felt like he was floating. He closed the door and wondered if everything inside would be normal if he opened it again. Maybe he happened to accidently step into an alternate reality for only a second.

"I told you not to go in there."

The woman's tone was snide and entrenched in sarcastic delight. Jake turned to face her, not sure of what to say until he saw the scene in the bathroom and decided he didn't need to say anything. The woman stood at the sink cutting lines from the significantly diminished pile of cocaine and a small, crimson trickle had started to peek from the side of her left nostril. Dark circles were pronounced prominently beneath her eyes and the little curl she had to her hair a moment before had gone straight from sweat and stuck in unflattering chunks to the sides of her head.

Beyond the sink, one of the men from the hallway sat on the toilet with his pants down while the other man knelt in front of him feverishly fellating. The man on his knees pulled his own penis from the front of his jeans and tapped on it like a flute while his other hand worked the first man's shaft. The woman snorted another generous helping of blow, and Jake turned from the bathroom to slowly make his way back down the hallway.

16

THE FEW HOURS OF SLEEP he'd gotten were plagued with nightmares and visions of evil, leaving him sweat-drenched and tangled in the sheets. He woke up dazed, wondering if the incidents from the previous night had really happened or if they were phantom memories lingering from nightmares. He had no doubt what he'd seen *was* absolutely real. What he didn't know was how he was going to get through the workday.

The dynamic at the facility had already shifted dramatically from what he was used to. He felt like he'd accidently stepped into a neighboring dimension with an entirely different timeline where things like fucking a dog-headed woman while someone watched and jerked off was commonplace.

It wasn't just *someone* jerking off, though. It was Max. Of all the insanity he'd witnessed at the party, seeing his best friend participating in—well, he didn't know what—was most troubling. He should have called out to him. He should have walked up, turned Max around in his chair regardless of the masturbating, and demanded to know what was going on. He should have gone into Paris's room to at least check on her. He should have . . .

Jake took a second to look at the numbers on his digital alarm clock, not wanting to believe what the particular arrangement of bright red lines was telling him. It was an hour later than his usual wakeup time. It wasn't like Jake to set his alarm wrong, but with the shape he was in last night, he was lucky he'd remembered to set it at all.

He looked from the clock to the broken phone next to it and realized he had no way of calling work to say he'd be late. He'd planned to pick a new phone up last night after he'd stopped by Max's, but nothing about the prior evening had gone according to plan. If he *really* wanted to, Jake could run down to the corner and use the phone at the deli, but he didn't want to do that. He was resigned to get there when he got there and accept whatever consequences there may be.

Jake poured himself from his bed to the floor with the slow smoothness of dripping sap. His mouth was dry and hot and tasted like he'd licked the bottom of a septic tank. His memory was fuzzy regarding details of the rest of the evening after what he'd seen in Max's room. He didn't remember drinking too much but his head and mouth told him different. He remembered sitting in his car after leaving the party but couldn't recall the drive home.

The clothes he'd worn the day before were strewn in a trail leading from the door to his bed. He picked each article up in the reverse order they'd been discarded, putting them back on as he went. Finding clean clothes to wear was too much of a chore. When he put on his pants, he found the half joint he'd saved in his pocket. Without hesitation he put it between his lips and lit it with a lighter from the other pocket.

He remembered the joint had been potent even for him, which made it the perfect cure for his hangover. He was no longer concerned with sharing it like he'd originally planned, knowing he'd need to smoke the rest of it to straighten out enough for work. Besides, the concern for his friend had mutated into anger, so sharing anything with Max had taken a backseat to his temper.

At least it was Friday and, assuming he made it through the day, Jake would have the weekend to get together with Max. He was mad at his friend but confident all would make sense when explained. At least, that's what he told himself.

Fully dressed, Jake circled the small apartment until he found his keys, which were, for whatever reason, in the kitchen sink. His wallet was still in the back pocket of his pants, so that was one less thing to worry about. He didn't see his hoodie anywhere obvious and didn't have time to look for it. He was pretty sure he'd left it in his car but, if not, he'd have to figure something out.

He hoped the facility had extra sweatshirts on hand for absent-minded employees who left home in a rush, or who may have blacked out after seeing a dog-headed woman fuck their boss while their best friend jerked off. If not, it would be a long and brutal day in The Box.

Jake smoked the rest of the joint on his way to the facility with the windows open only a crack. He wasn't concerned with smelling like weed at work anymore after what he saw last night. If someone took issue, Jake figured he could use what he saw at the party as a means to avoid trouble *if* Tim said anything about it at all.

Or could he? It was possible Tim's behavior was common knowledge, along with whatever was going on with the dog-headed Elise, and was deemed acceptable among the rest of the facility's employees. Even so, if activities like what he'd witnessed were the norm, then smoking weed shouldn't even be a blip on their radar. Especially since it was his direct supervisor who'd given him the joint he was currently smoking.

He didn't know Tim well enough to get a read on him and couldn't tell if the man was being sarcastic when reminding Jake about the random drug testing policy while passing a joint. Jake didn't discount the possibility Tim had been testing him, setting him up for the ultimate fall while surreptitiously letting him know he was doing it.

Jake waited at the last traffic light before the entrance to the parking lot of the facility and thought about the possible scenario he may be walking into. He imagined Tim waiting at the front door to greet him, holding out a small plastic cup, which would be an unnecessary formality. He'd fail the drug test, of course, and Tim knew it.

Jake was starting to wonder why he was transferred in the first place and now wished he'd been among the Fam-Mark employees who'd been let go. Having to work two shitty jobs to make ends meet was starting to look appealing up against the insane confusion of the facility, but he wasn't ready to jump ship just yet. It was only his third day, and Jake wasn't going to be deterred by the "quirky" behavior of his new coworkers.

He knew using quirky was a stretch, but in this case the term helped to compartmentalize Tim's and Elise's actions at the party, keeping them separate from the Tim and Elise he worked with. While flimsy at best, this was how Jake chose to deal with things for the time being. He wanted to stick it out for at least a week, and he very badly needed to talk to Max, hoping his friend could explain the "quirky" behavior. He needed Max to make it make sense.

He was counting on it.

The rest of the joint proved just as powerful, leaving Jake stoned enough to not realize he was the only person walking down the hall. The day before, when he ran into Elise and dropped his pizza, it had been crowded with employees going and coming, but today he hadn't passed a single person.

Granted, he was late, but it wasn't like he was lurking the halls of a high school while class was in session, hoping not to get caught without a pass. There were several different departments, all with offices scattered across the entire facility along with all the production rooms, but there was no way every single person just so happened to be doing their jobs all at the same time. Was there?

With no other stimuli to distract him, Jake couldn't help but focus on the red stripe. It lined both walls, making it inescapable to his peripheral vision on either side, and no matter how hard he focused on staring straight ahead he could still see it.

He rounded the corner on his way into the locker room and, still, the hall remained empty. There was no one coming toward the locker room from the other direction either.

A dark, chaotic energy made the air around him feel scratchy and stiff like the tiny groupings of thorns that sneak through the nubs of young, budding succulents. It left invisible, ghostly abrasions on his exposed arms and face as he pushed through the door to the locker room. Jake expected to find it as empty as the hall and, as he took his third step, the door swung open behind him only half a second after.

He whirled around and found himself disoriented from being caught off guard. Moments earlier, there hadn't been a single soul in the hall as far as Jake could see, yet standing at the door now was Tim. He held it open with one hand, the red bracelet dangling prominently from his wrist.

The memory of a dog-headed Elise wearing the red collar around her neck with the attached leash held tightly in Tim's grip flashed across the screen of Jake's mind's eye. The supervisor beckoned to Jake with his other hand, using all four fingers to perform the gesture.

"Hey, Jake, I'm glad I caught you before you changed."

Tim was smiling in the same creepy way he did at the party, and the implied sentiment of the expression clashed uncomfortably with the negatively charged atmosphere. The gears in Jake's head spun dangerously fast as he tried and failed to solve the puzzle of where Tim had come from.

He could have sprinted from the shadows at the far end of the hall as Jake stepped across the threshold and, while this was the most plausible theory his brain could conjure from the limited data available, it was flimsy and easy to refute. Tim wasn't breathing hard, his face wasn't flush from a sudden burst of exertion, and his forehead and neck were perspiration free.

"Would you follow me down to my office, please?"

"S-Sure," Jake stuttered, his mouth having gone completely dry.

He nodded to reiterate his compliance, but Tim had already let go of the door and turned around. Jake reached out to catch it but the door slipped past the tips of his fingers and closed. He fumbled with the handle, taking a beat longer than it should have to open back up. Tim was already ten feet down the hall by the time Jake stumbled out, and he jogged to catch up.

Jake walked up beside Tim but remained a half step behind. He hoped he wouldn't have to turn and run from the man, but if the need arose suddenly, Jake would have the advantage of a head start, albeit small. The atmosphere became constrictive and jagged as they walked toward Tim's office, like it was ground zero for the cause of the disruption.

Only, it wasn't.

It was close though. A prickly, creeping vine sprouted from his cottonmouth and lazily snaked its way down Jake's throat with the tender gentleness of a pipe cleaner being shoved through a dick hole. Jake moved his tongue around in his mouth, hoping the motion might coax saliva from his glands. Instead, it acted like a dry mop, managing to suck up the small bit of moisture left between his teeth.

Upon entering Tim's office, the claustrophobia-inducing air thinned out some. It was much warmer than in the hallway, and Jake felt dampness at the center of his tongue begin to spread out, returning some wetness to his mouth. It wasn't much but would at least allow him to speak and comment on whatever the impromptu meeting happened to be about.

Jake's heart was in his throat, pounding with an intensity he feared would burst the arteries in his neck and separate his head from his body. He imagined his head detaching and falling forward into his lap, a tremendous geyser of blood erupting from his neck to create the effect of a fountain composed of gore being the final thing his eyes registered. As the final darkness eternally eclipsed his vision, he would see Tim and the dog-headed Elise holding chunks of torn flesh on spits into the rushing, warm, crimson tidal wave.

"Take a seat please, Jacob."

Jake realized he was standing next to the chair across the desk from Tim and quickly stepped over to sit down.

"I'm afraid I have some bad news," Tim continued.

Jake tried to swallow but didn't have enough saliva to do so, and a dry crackling sound accompanied the spasm in his throat. He expected Tim to hand him a cup across the desk to take the drug test they both knew he'd fail. Jake dropped his hands to his lap to keep the supervisor from seeing how badly they'd begun to shake, not just from nerves, but anger at the thought of being set up.

"I thought maybe someone caught you in the parking lot and let you know before you made it in, but I guess you're just"—Tim paused and made a show of looking at his watch, which was flanked on each side by a red bracelet—"really fucking late."

Jake had forgotten he was late for a moment until Tim reminded him with an expletive attached for emphasis. Had his boss actually just said *fucking* late? He replayed the line in his head trying to decipher from Tim's tone if he was being "casual" like at the party or was really pissed off.

"Anyway," Tim went on, not giving Jake a chance to comment on, or apologize for his tardiness. "In lieu of the surrounding circumstances, I'll overlook it this time."

"Circumstances?"

Jake was surprised by the inadvertent escape of the first word he'd spoken since leaving the locker room and, with it, the air turned heavy around him again. He was starting to get the sense these *circumstances* were responsible for the inescapable feeling of dread woven into the atmosphere of the facility.

"There was an . . . accident earlier this morning toward the end of the night shift. Sadly, Ivan was killed while working in The Box."

"What? Killed?"

Jake didn't even know there was an overnight shift in the first place, although it made sense, since the facility ran twenty-four hours a day. What didn't make sense was why Ivan was working said shift? Jake had seen him at the party drinking and who knows what else. The man couldn't even string a coherent sentence together, so what was he doing working period, let alone on the night shift in The Box?

"Yes." Tim looked solemn for the first time since Jake had been with him. "It occurred while loading the day's product out into the trucks. Ivan apparently hadn't been paying close enough attention to his surroundings and drove his forklift off the loading dock. He tried to jump out but was tangled in the machinery. Ivan was impaled by one of the forks through the neck."

"Jesus . . ." Jake finally managed.

"He was decapitated, I'm afraid, but at the very least we can take solace knowing his death was quick and Ivan felt no pain."

Jake didn't know how you could have your head cut off by a forklift and not feel any pain. People always say quick, instant deaths are painless, but he never took stock in that theory.

There was no way anyone could *truly* know how it feels until you actually die, but then you can't share your findings. Jake believed dying did hurt no matter how it happened, and only going through the actual experience could change his mind.

"I'm sure you noticed the facility was like a ghost town on your way to the locker room," Tim went on. "We've closed for the day and through the weekend for the routine accident investigation. The Box will have to be deep cleaned and sanitized, and then approved by the city's health department before business can resume as usual. Didn't you notice the parking lot was practically empty when you were walking up? You must have been *really* out of it."

Tim winked and mimed smoking a joint by pinching his thumb and forefinger together against his lips. Jake had no idea how to take the remark and gesture, especially when presented against the backdrop of a serious topic.

"Wa—Wasn't Ivan at Max's party last night?" Jake's voice was slowly returning to full strength.

Tim leaned back in his chair, keeping his palms on the desk while squinting up at the ceiling like he was doing his impression of what he thought a person trying to recall information looked like. He even rocked a few times and clicked his tongue against the roof of his mouth for good measure and to give his character depth.

"Ivan at Max's? I don't recall seeing him there, but I didn't end up staying very long. Rest assured the investigation will include a blood test to reveal what, if any, substances Ivan had in his system, as well as the presence of alcohol.

"I would be very surprised if anything showed up though. Ivan was pretty straight-laced and never displayed any behavior to arouse suspicion he may have had a drug or drinking problem."

Jake's brain severed its connection to his mouth to keep him from making the mistake of commenting on Tim's explanation. The situation Jake found himself in was not going to benefit from asking questions, and he suddenly wanted to get away very badly; away from the conversation, away from Tim's office, and far, far away from the facility.

"That's basically the long and short of it." Tim pushed away from his desk and stood. "So, head home and enjoy the three-day weekend. We'll be having mandatory safety training first thing Monday."

Jake stood, wanting to make his exit quickly, but couldn't ignore the hand Tim was holding out for him to shake. The slack hanging from his red bracelet was tied into three knots evenly spaced along the cord. The one closest to his wrist was bigger than the next one down, which was bigger than the one closest to the bottom.

He grabbed Tim's hand, gave it a quick shake, and headed for the door. If the facility was closed, Max would have to be home, and Jake needed an explanation from his friend to answer the growing list of questions he was racking up.

"Oh, Jacob, by the way," Tim called out, prompting Jake to turn back around before making his escape. "Max is upstairs attending executive training for his new position. There are still a handful of office folks who will be working their regular hours. I figured you might stop by his place on your way home, and I wanted to save you the trip."

"Save me the trip?"

"Yes, and his sister is very sick, from what I understand, so I'm sure you wouldn't want to disturb her."

"Training?"

"That's right." Tim smiled and reached down, plucking the receiver from the phone's base on his desk with one hand, and punched at the keypad with the other. "I'm sure he'll tell you all about it the next time you see him."

Tim put the phone to his ear and gave Jake a *get the fuck out of my office* nod, which he was more than happy to do. Despite wanting to ask, Jake knew Tim wasn't going to give him the answers he needed and, to be honest, he was starting to think Max wasn't going to either.

He walked quickly down the hall and started running once he rounded the corner. He sprinted all the way to the front door and out into the parking lot where he slowed and came to a full stop, trying to catch his breath as he looked around at the near empty parking lot. Aside from his silver Civic, only two or three other cars dotted the vast and desolate expanse of cement.

Jake was high and preoccupied when he came in but couldn't believe he would have such extreme tunnel vision to the extent he didn't notice the empty lot. He bent over with his hands on his knees, hoping the change in position would allow more oxygen into his lungs.

His toes were barely touching the red line and, just as he suspected, with no cars to block his view, Jake could see it run the width of the lot then curve around the side of the building.

17

JAKE PLUGGED IN THE NEW phone he'd bought as soon as he arrived back at the apartment, but hadn't used it yet. For the last forty-five minutes he'd been going through boxes of books and miscellaneous junk from his old room back home. The apartment was too small to display most of these items, so they stayed packed away in a closet until he either moved to a bigger place or decided to get rid of them.

Looking through it now, Jake found most of it to be garbage he wasn't sure why he'd decided to keep, but now wasn't the time to start sorting trash. Seeing the three knots tied in the slack dangling from Tim's bracelet sparked an old memory from the deep recesses of Jake's mind, only he didn't realize it until he was halfway home.

Jake's immediate family wasn't religious when he was growing up, although his grandparents on both sides were. Their devoutness was no doubt the reason Jake's mother and father not only didn't participate in religious activities, but also why they rallied against the institution, not wanting the concept to have an influence on Jake.

Because of this Jake had only a vague awareness of what the Devil was supposed to be, but any additional information on the subject came from watching horror movies and the various role-playing games he and his friends participated in. They'd started with Dungeons and Dragons, which he and his friends played for what was nearly their entire waking life one summer.

Jake wrote countless campaigns, and eventually he and his group moved on to try different D & D-style games released on the wave of the original's popularity. They were unimpressed with the first few they tried, finding the gameplay too rigid, as well as lacking in an overall imaginative direction. He was going to suggest they revisit their old favorite D & D campaigns until he received an impromptu gift from his mother one afternoon.

She'd been out running errands and came upon a new role-playing, campaign-based game called Mage of the Hellmouth, and bought it for Jake and his gang of role-playing pals to take for a spin. She never gave a specific reason as to why she bought the game and Jake, happy for the present, didn't ask for one. The boys immediately began devouring every bit of information the game included as Jake's mother left the basement to put groceries away and get dinner started.

The aspect of the game that stuck out most to them was, while in other games, Hell was mentioned or even minimally included, Mage of the Hellmouth featured Hell exclusively. They weren't disappointed because the game's world was huge and would allow for hours of unique gameplay, all of it taking place within, or just outside, the gates of Hell.

The game was complicated, having a lot of options and characters included. A broad overview of the storyline involved a powerful Mage who'd gained access to the Hellmouth, the entrance to Hell from Earth, and was able to channel its evil energy into his magic. The Mage's objective was, of course, to take over the world and also Hell. Players could choose to be one of the many servants of Hell trying to sever the Mage's link to the dark powers and use them instead to destroy him.

Players could also be a servant of the Mage, with their objective being to beat back the servants of Hell while working to strengthen their master's hold on the Hellmouth's power. Strangely enough, these were the only two choices.

There were other characters involved and, while not playable, they performed an integral part in the game. These were warriors, barbarians, knights, and rogue magicians who were constantly launching attacks at the Mage from the topside, or "Earth."

Every other turn or so, the Mage would be attacked by one of these groups, which slowed down or prevented the progress of the players. While this could be frustrating at times, it made for satisfyingly longer gameplay.

There was one specific campaign Jake remembered playing, the one he was searching through boxes in his closet for, that had something to do with spells involving knots. He was playing as a servant of the Mage during this particular game when his current mission changed due to an attack launched by demons.

It seemed they had released a great and powerful beast from the depths of Hell who was heading for the Hellmouth to destroy the Mage. In turn, the Mage tasked his team of servants to scour Hell to find three lengths of red cord. Jake took a beating finding them, and his character was near death when he delivered each cord to his master.

The Mage rewarded Jake's character by restoring his health and increasing his magical ability before tying a different-sized knot in each length of red rope. The knots worked a special magic to bind the power of the beast sent to attack, rendering the creature harmless. Later in this particular game, the Mage would fuse the knotted ropes into a single length, which allowed him to control the hellish beast, turning it back on those who released it.

This wasn't the only time a spell involving knots was used in a campaign but, the one Jake was searching for, the one he was reminded of earlier in the day, depended on their magic exclusively. The reason this campaign stuck with Jake was because of how long it took to complete all the required tasks, collect all the necessary objects, and make sure to do it all in the correct order.

These steps were required to be completed before the Mage could fuse the separate, knotted ropes to take control of the beast and its great power. Apparently this was the last bit of leverage needed to give the Mage dominion over Hell, which finally ended the game.

A mess of loose paper, books, and magazines encircled Jake, pushing their way farther out across the floor with every box he emptied. He pulled another box from the pile, pulled up the flaps, and stuck his hand in. He could tell, when his fingers made contact with the contents, he'd found what he was looking for.

When he pulled his hand back out it was full of campaign booklets, and a glance inside confirmed the rest of the box was nothing but. Jake set the box on the floor, knelt beside it, and starting sorting through the books. A shrill chirp smashed the quiet stillness of the apartment and startled Jake into ducking down against the box for cover.

The chirp stopped, but only for a beat before it resumed buzz sawing through the silence like the sound was holding a grudge. By the third chirp Jake realized it was his new phone. It sounded nothing like his old one, and the foreign ringing scared the bejeezus out of him. He felt like an idiot, but at least no one was there to see him jump.

Jake stepped gingerly across the minefield of junk he'd have to scoop back into boxes and forget about for another ten years as he made his way to the phone.

"Hello?"

There was no reply as the odor from the new plastic off-gassing filled his nose.

"Hello?" he repeated.

"J-Jake."

The voice on the other end sounded weak and far away, but Jake still recognized it.

"Jake." A pause for a breath, then "Help."

It was Paris.

18

JAKE SPED TO MAX AND Paris's apartment, running more than one red light along the way. Luckily, a space was open for him to park in front of their building, but he'd been prepared to double park if necessary. He leapt from the car, almost forgetting his keys, but he caught the door before it shut behind him, removed them from the ignition, and jammed them into his pocket.

He sprinted through the complex. His heart pounded way too hard and fast for running such a short distance. When he rounded the corner and approached the apartment, his fast-beating heart leapt up into his throat and stopped. His heart hung out of place for an eternal moment before dropping down into his stomach, not unlike a car's transmission falling out the bottom after being violently thrown out of gear.

The door to the apartment was open.

It wasn't wide open. The inside edge of the door pressed up against the strike plate in the doorframe but wasn't closed enough to catch. It was like someone left in a hurry, pulling the door closed behind them without realizing it hadn't shut all the way.

Jake went for the doorknob but stopped when he saw the red bracelet from the night before lying on the sidewalk at his feet. Only now, the bracelet was untied, making it just a loose piece of braided, red cord.

"She's not in there anymore."

Jake hadn't heard the neighbor open her door and had no idea how long she'd been standing there. Something about the way she looked at him made Jake feel like he'd been caught doing something wrong. Her name was Vanessa or Veronica? Jake couldn't remember, but he did remember she was a massive bitch to Max and Paris.

"What?"

It was all he could say. The two sudden disruptions to his momentum in such close succession made Jake feel like a stalled-out dragster unable to get off the line without throwing a rod or blowing a cylinder.

"I assume you're here for what's her name," the neighbor said with the warmth of an undertaker.

"Paris?"

"Yeah, her."

Jake waited for the woman to continue, but instead she chewed the inside of her cheek while staring blankly past him.

"What happened to her? Where did she go?"

"How should I know?" Her tone was flippant, impatient. "I was trying to sit outside and read when some guys ran up, unlocked the door, and ran inside. A minute later they came out propping her up. They pretty much carried her to their truck."

"And you didn't think this was out of the ordinary? You didn't think you should call the police?" Jake struggled to control his shaking with each word.

"I don't know what kind of freaky shit that bitch is into." She spat the words in Jake's face. "You should have seen the party they had here last night!"

Jake knew he wasn't going to get far with the neighbor, but he didn't think she knew much else anyway.

"Fine," he said. "You said they took her to a truck. What kind of truck was it?"

"That's the freaky part," she said. "It looked exactly like an old ice cream truck."

19

JAKE STOOD OUTSIDE OF THE partially ajar door to Max and Paris's apartment for several minutes trying to decide what to do. Vanessa or Valerie or whatever the hell her name was resumed her "resting bitch face" after the ice cream truck remark. She cast one final judgmental glare Jake's way before stepping inside and shutting her door without another word.

Jake was conflicted, confused, exhausted, and close to being fed up with the whole situation. He vacillated on what course of action to take, trying to decide whether to get involved or not. He could go inside and look around, or he could pull the door shut, go back to his apartment to sleep, and hope everything took care of itself. His emotions slipped past concern into anger, and his fingers tightened into fists while his jaw inadvertently clenched and unclenched.

He didn't want to look down. He didn't want to acknowledge the thing that kept him standing there, and the reason he knew he *had* to go in to investigate. He bent over and scooped up the untied bracelet, tucking it into the front pocket of his jeans as he pushed the door open. It was dark and the air was still, stale, and thick with lonely silence. Despite the overwhelming feeling he was indeed alone, he couldn't help but call out.

"Hello? Paris? Are you in here? Max?"

He stood just inside the open door and used his heel to keep it from closing all the way. He lingered, listening for a response or even an echo, of which came neither. He didn't realize he'd balled his hands into fists again until he stepped all the way into the apartment and went to close the door behind him. He relaxed his fingers and wiped the sweat from his palms on the front of his jeans. With the door closed, the silence thickened around him, becoming impossibly quieter, like the room had suddenly become pressurized.

Being in the apartment felt like being in a vacuum where time moved differently, and the rules of reality as Jake knew them did not necessarily apply. The air wasn't oxygenated enough for him to breathe, and he found himself hyperventilating while trying to fill his lungs. He couldn't leave now though. Despite no one answering his calls, Jake had to take a look around to be sure the apartment was indeed empty.

The first step felt like he was moving his leg through deep, thick mud or quickly hardening concrete. The second step was a little easier and, by the third, he felt acclimated enough to navigate the atmosphere at a regular pace. With things seeming to normalize around him, Jake was assaulted with residual evidence from the party lingering within random pockets of air unevenly spaced.

The aroma of sour beer, stale smoke, and the commingling of sweat, perfume, and body odor peppered the living room like he was walking past a uniquely bizarre cosmetics counter. There were no lights on but what filtered through the closed blinds was enough for Jake to see the state of the room. Empty cans and bottles filled nearly every available space atop the coffee and end table, along with small groupings of trash scattered across random spots on the floor.

While the scene perfectly captured the aftermath of a party, it wasn't consistent with the way Max and Paris kept their apartment. They weren't obsessive about cleanliness, but rather geared their focus on tidiness. There was a place for everything and everything was in its place. The shelf may be covered in an inch of dust but everything on it was exactly where it was supposed to be. Also, neither of them would ever allow a drink on the coffee table without a coaster. Jake couldn't let himself fall down the rabbit hole of things not making sense, or he would be distracted for hours.

"Paris," he called, turning to head down the hall. "Paris, are you here? Are you okay?"

He didn't expect a response, but hearing his own voice out loud was an unexpected comfort that helped drive him forward. Paris's door was shut. Jake stepped up, knocked, and opened the door quickly without allowing time for a response or for him to lose his nerve.

Paris wasn't in the room, but he didn't expect her to be. Her bed was stripped down to the fitted sheet with the comforter and pillows tangled in a heap against the far wall. The room smelled like sick. Vomit as well as other bodily fluids had obviously been expelled recently within, and Jake suspected the pile of blankets, or rather what was *in* the pile, was the source.

He suddenly felt like he was invading Paris's privacy, and she would most likely be mortified to know he had been in the room after it was left in such a state. He stepped back into the hall and closed the door behind him. He looked down the hall toward the bathroom and Max's room. Both doors were closed.

The scenes he encountered in each of those rooms the prior evening were still freshly tattooed in his mind, and Jake suspected they'd stay with him for quite some time. He didn't want to venture any farther. He didn't want to look in those rooms but, again, he knew he had to. The sound of shrapnel spinning in a rock tumbler cleaved the heavy, fetid air, startling Jake to the extent he nearly covered his head and hit the deck. The noise stopped for a second and sounded again as he realized it was the sound of the phone ringing in the kitchen.

He'd never answered the phone at Max's apartment before but, in the moment, he felt obligated and headed back down the hall. The kitchen was in far worse shape than the rest of the apartment, which made him wonder what the bathroom looked like, but he was still glad he didn't check.

The refrigerator was hanging open, and an open beer lying on its side was visible from where Jake stood. This explained the jaundice-yellow puddle on the floor in front of the fridge, but for the puke in the sink and three and a half burnt pieces of bread in a frying pan on the stove, there was no explanation.

The phone bleated a garbled, piercing call for attention again, and Jake quickly yanked the receiver from the wall beside him.

"H-Hello?"

He almost tacked on *Jenkins' residence* like he was the wise-ass neighbor kid answering his friend's parents' phone in an early nineties sitcom.

"Jake? Jake, is that you? I thought you'd be there."

It was Max. Jake nearly let the phone slide from his head into the sink-vomit but managed to hang on. That was the last voice he expected to hear.

"Max? Where the hell are you? Where's Paris? She called me for he—"

"Whoa, whoa, whoa, slow down, buddy," Max interrupted. "Paris is fine. She caught what I had and let herself get a little too dehydrated. Once they put an I.V. in her, she perked right up."

"Wait, what? Who put an I.V. in her? H-how did you know to call me at your apartment?"

Jake's head was starting to spin, and he legitimately felt like he might pass out. He leaned his shoulder against the wall in a patch of something sticky and started to take long, slow breaths.

"Paris told me she thought she remembered calling you for help, but was so out of it she thought she might have dreamed it."

Max's tone had the mysterious quality of words being said through a smile, and Jake was starting to think his friend was laughing at the intensity of his concern.

"I called your apartment a few times, and when you didn't answer I thought you might have come over and somehow gotten in to the apartment. And I was right!"

"The door was open," Jake said, the dizziness lifting. "I just walked in."

"The door was open?"

"Yeah," Jake replied a little too quickly. "I guess it didn't get closed all the way when *they* came to take Paris away."

Jake hoped the emphasis would prompt Max to tell him exactly who took Paris and where. It didn't.

"That makes sense." Max rattled off the response without a thought. "Look, you sound upset, and I can tell you're a little freaked out."

"Oh, you can tell?"

Jake spat his frustration through the receiver, envisioning it traveling through the lines and coming out the other side to sock his friend in the eye.

"I promise I can explain everything."

"I'm listening."

"Not right now," Max whined, "but soon. Go to your apartment, and I'll call you there tonight by seven."

"What? Call me tonight?"

"By seven," he reiterated.

Jake wasn't in the mood to argue, and the various smells in the apartment had begun to mix into a sickening potpourri.

"Fine," Jake finally said. "But by seven!"

"I promise, buddy. I've got to go now, but I'll call you tonight. Oh, and Jake?"

"Yeah?"

"Don't touch my stash."

The line went dead, and Jake pulled the receiver from his ear, staring at the thing like he'd never seen a phone in his life. He slammed it down on the counter, snapping it in half and sending sharp, pointy pieces of plastic across the kitchen in dozens of fun sizes.

He walked from the kitchen to the end table in the living room and opened the drawer on the front. Inside was a metal tin in the shape of a bus that at one time housed animal crackers, but now it was where Max kept his weed. He grabbed the tin and left the drawer open.

On his way out he thought about leaving the door open, but instead gained a modicum of satisfaction by slamming it behind him as hard as he could.

20

JAKE DIDN'T GO STRAIGHT HOME from Max and Paris's apartment. He hadn't planned to divert from his path but, as he pulled away from the curb, he remembered something he hadn't thought of in years. It was like a switch flipped in the back of his brain to reconnect severed synapses, otherwise corroded into uselessness from years of punishing substance abuse.

In the old facility where he and Max worked less than a week ago there were framed pictures hung along the hall past the entrance of the building. The pictures were from the very early stages of the Fam-Mark company, depicting how far they'd come since the beginning. There were pictures of the first machines the company used when they only needed four people total to work the entire production line.

There were a few candid shots of employees working in the production room, an exterior shot of the building with the original, much smaller sign, but the detail Jake suddenly recalled was in the background of pictures from the first outdoor promotions the company put on.

Back then, Fam-Mark employees would set up sample booths in parks and grocery store parking lots. They gave the whole thing a picnic-like vibe and apparently these guerilla-style sampling events were key to the company's initial success.

Part of the quaint presentation was an old-fashioned ice cream truck. Most of the time it sat parked off to the side as an extravagant set piece, but occasionally the truck became the center of attention when they would serve directly from it. Something about the way the neighbor said *ice cream truck* compelled Jake's brain to sift through whatever useless excuses for memories he kept on top of the pile to find the image of that truck.

It wasn't hard for Jake to correct his route and a single left turn later he was headed to the old facility. He didn't expect to find the actual truck there and had, in fact, never seen it outside of a photograph. He thought maybe seeing the photos again would concretely confirm his suspicions and possibly reveal some bit of information he'd yet to realize.

He wouldn't know until he went to check it out.

There was always a chance he'd created a false memory because he wanted to believe there was a link between Fam-Mark and what happened to Paris. What if there wasn't an ice cream truck in the pictures at all? What if it was another type of vehicle, or no vehicle at all?

Jake thought he was generally a pretty sharp guy, but he smoked a lot of weed and was never completely sober while at work, or ever really. He'd fought tooth and nail with people in the past over supposed facts he swore to be true and even went as far as to claim he'd been witness to many things that turned out never to have happened.

Sometimes the brain can convince itself an event took place, or an experience occurred, when it never actually did. It would even concoct specialized and intricate details to further confuse the person into thinking something happened to them when, in fact, it had not. The memory was a tricky rascal in that way, and the kind of tricks it plays can make it damn hard to trust even an eyewitness. This is why Jake had to go to the old facility and see if any part of his memory was accurate.

Jake turned down the street, surprised by how different the block was now. The area was primarily industrial, populated with warehouses, machine shops, and food production facilities like Fam-Mark. There were always delivery trucks coming and going, especially at this time of day, as well as the general tangle of cars and trucks parked up and down both sides of the street further complicating things for the truck drivers.

This morning the street was empty save for a few scattered trucks belonging to a paint company, but they were a ways down past Fam-Mark. So far, in fact, they may as well not have been there at all for as much difference as they made. Jake momentarily entertained a possibility where the entire industry sector closed for the day in solidarity with Fam-Mark regarding the accident.

Jake knew that couldn't be the case, but he honestly had no other guess as to why the other businesses on the block were closed. It wasn't a holiday. There was no inclimate weather or disaster in any other form that would warrant closing businesses. The temperature had been gradually dropping over the last two weeks with the arrival of fall, but the block had already taken on a cold and colorless harsh edge typically seen during the bleakest part of winter.

He couldn't remember if there were leaves on the trees when he drove by at the beginning of the week, but they were completely bare now, without a trace of the fallen leaves on the street or sidewalk. He was distracted by how deserted the street was and almost drove past the old facility, but caught himself in time to swing the Civic into the parking lot at the last second.

He absently pulled his car into a space out of habit, despite the lot being empty. It was hard to break the unspoken social contract of parking etiquette even when it clearly did not apply. He put the car back in drive to move it closer to the facility's entrance when he noticed another car in the lot. It was a blue Ford Fiesta parked in the space closest to the door. Rob's blue Ford Fiesta.

From across the lot, the car looked dirty, but not extraordinarily so. Rob was never one to keep his vehicle squeaky-clean, so Jake didn't give it a thought until he pulled up next to it. From this proximity, it was obvious the car had been there for several days.

A layer of dust had settled on the windows but was only thick enough to slightly obscure Jake's view into the car. The only items visible to him was a box of tissues in the center console and a book called *Being the Best Darn Me* on the passenger seat. A pink stickynote peeked from the top of the book to mark his place, indicating Rob hadn't gotten very far in his self-help journey.

Surprisingly, there were no leaves on or underneath the car but, since there weren't any leaves anywhere, Jake figured whoever cleaned them up would have removed them from the car as well. He walked around to the driver side and managed to stop short of stepping in a slimy, black puddle pushing out from beneath the vehicle.

Rob mentioned his car had a slow oil leak a few weeks back. He was talking to some of the more mechanically inclined employees about it in the break room one day, asking if they had suggestions for a cheap, quick fix he could do on his own. What he really wanted was to persuade one of them to fix it for him, but Rob didn't quite grasp the nuance required when dropping hints.

He was able to give orders and direction when it came to his job as a managing supervisor, but the art of effortlessly inserting subtle suggestions into conversation was far beyond his wheelhouse. Jake was well aware of people who were only able to communicate in one specific way to every single person they encounter whether the person is responsive to it or not.

He'd met a few people like this in his life so far, like the manager of the grocery store he worked in when he'd freshly turned sixteen, and the Algebra 2 teacher from his senior year with the social skills of a comatose sea-slug. Both communicated through yelling commands and chastising failure.

These men were the reason Jake realized the importance of tailoring the way he interacted with someone in order to get the best and most pleasant response. The whole "ruling with an iron fist" routine was antiquated and unproductive, but a hard behavior for the old guard to let go of.

No one volunteered to help Rob, or give him any suggestions, and when he left the break room, the group laughed while mocking their supervisor's awkward attempt at soliciting their help. Judging by the size of the sludgy puddle, it was safe to assume Rob still hadn't convinced someone to fix it for him. It was also a telltale sign the car had most likely been there a while, since it was only supposed to be a "slow" leak.

The idea Rob's car was still there because it had broken down the last day the facility was open seemed the most logical scenario, but Jake had a feeling the true reason was far from logical. He stepped back from the car, folded his arms across his chest and stared at the blue piece-of-shit while he thought.

Despite having spent so much time there, nothing about the entire area felt familiar now. It was like the last night of a long running play had come and gone and a crew already stripped the stage down to build scenery for an entirely new production. The air smelled of ozone, as if laced with enough electricity to slowly cook his insides.

Jake turned to look up the steps leading to the door of the facility, unable to figure out why it now seemed so foreign to him. The Fam-Mark sign was still above the door, but even it lacked the life it had held as he walked under it day after day. He equated the feeling to trying to talk to his grandmother with Alzheimer's as she struggled to remember who he was. The intangible welcoming element the sign once possessed was stripped away and replaced with a foreboding feeling of danger.

Without realizing he'd walked up the steps, Jake found himself standing inches from the door, the heavily tinted glass making it impossible for him to see inside. Knowing it would be locked, he still brought his fingers to the handle and pulled. Surprisingly, it opened, and without the resistance he expected he stumbled back, nearly falling. Keeping his hold on the handle was what helped him regain his balance and kept him from stepping off the edge.

Now solidly on his feet, Jake stepped one foot into the darkness while holding the door open so the majority of his body was outside in case he needed to make a quick break for it. He didn't know what would prompt him to run but, with the block drenched in a syrupy-thick eeriness, he wasn't going to take any chances.

"Hello?"

Jake called into the darkness, answered only by the echo and followed closely by the smell of stale, uncirculated air mixed with the faint aroma of spoiled meat. With the air conditioners off and the bay doors closed up, there was no way for the air to circulate. This was probably how the facility always truly smelled, but its scent was buried deep beneath the myriad constantly changing elements.

"Hello?" He gave it one more try, and then added, "Rob? Are you in here?"

Jake waited an extra beat before he decided to go in but, when he reached his hand to flip the light switch, nothing happened. He figured they wouldn't keep the electricity on, but thought it would take a week or two before the city cut it off. Without the lights, there was no use in him going to look at the pictures in the hall.

He stepped back and took a look around for something he could use to prop the door open. He spotted four cinderblocks stacked on the ground against the side of the loading dock. He was down the stairs and back up with one of the blocks, trying to work as fast as he could before losing his nerve. He pulled on the door again and opened it as far as it could go without breaking the mechanism.

Jake placed the cinderblock down in front of the door. He stepped back to take another look inside. The light allowed by the wide-open door sliced the darkness inside like a Bowie knife—sharp, precise, creating separation.

Dust danced through the sliver beam like sparks escaping upward from a bonfire, and Jake took a step inside but waited until his eyes adjusted to the limited light. A minute later, familiar shapes came into focus.

The light beam hit the far wall, climbed down to the hallway, and spilt across the ceiling. Jake was able to see better by the second and, based on the path the light took, he determined it would be enough to see what he came there to see. He stepped quickly but carefully through the small entryway on his way to the hall. He wanted to get in and out quickly without injuring himself, particularly since he was alone.

Jake was familiar enough with the inside of the facility, but the place was full of heavy machinery and equipment, which could make things tricky in the dark. Rob told him they were dismantling machines the day the facility was closing, so there was the possibility of new obstacles left behind he would need to keep an eye out for. The pictures started three feet into the hall and continued nearly the entire length down. The ones with the ice cream truck he wanted to see were toward the end.

The first pictures were of the original Fam-Mark logo, followed by variations from the few times it changed over the years, which wasn't much. Next came a picture of the first facility with a very modest Fam-Mark sign hung proudly above the entrance.

Pictures of the first workers involved in the company came next, with the ones he came to see still up ahead, but Jake suddenly stopped. In that moment, he wasn't sure if he could make it any farther, or ever move from where he stood.

He saw it right away.

The photograph was one he'd glanced at everyday as he came and left work, but now it took on a whole new horrifyingly chilling significance. The still, stale atmosphere suddenly thinned around him, making his head start to spin. He reached his hand out to the wall beside the photo and leaned to keep from losing his balance.

The only thing different was the style of glasses and absence of an ever-present lab coat, but every other detail was spot on, from the red bracelets and necklace down to the striking resemblance to The Baroness Jake projected on her. It was Elise.

The photo had been taken at a party to celebrate the first run of product coming out of the facility, or at least that's what was engraved into a small piece of metal on the wall beneath it. There were people milling around in the background smiling, shaking hands, forever frozen holding up a drink mid-toast. The photo's intention was for Elise and the man she was with to be the prominent subject, but they'd been framed slightly off center to capture the candid exuberance happening behind them.

The man in the photo was Tim, and the smile on his face was posed to mock Jake in this very moment specifically from years in the past. Down the hall and around the corner came the sound of a phone ringing, and suddenly it wasn't silent anymore.

21

THE PHONE CONTINUED TO RING while Jake stood in the doorway of Rob's old office not wanting what he was seeing to be real. Nothing in the past few days of his life made any sense, including the scene before him.

When the phone started ringing a few minutes prior, the sound broke Jake from the shock he'd gone into over the photo. He'd felt overwhelmingly compelled to follow the sound down the hall, but allowed himself a brief stop when he reached the photos he'd come to see. He was happy his memory hadn't betrayed him and the old-time ice cream truck was in the pictures, just as he'd remembered.

Knowing he was right about the truck in the photos didn't provide him with any other clues as he'd hoped. He was going on a hunch and the confirmation proved only to further complicate the situation, but not as much as what lay before him.

At first glance, it looked like a harmless garment draped across the front of Rob's chair. If one was walking by and caught a quick look, they would take it for one of those beaded, ergonomic mats people put on their chairs because they've been duped into thinking it helps their back. An even shorter glimpse might not register anything at all.

A week ago, Jake would have thought it was nothing more than a slightly elaborate Halloween costume still under construction. It took a full twenty seconds for him to realize he was actually looking at Rob, or what was left of him. His eyes were gone from the sockets, leaving behind shallow black flesh-pockets in a flattened head attached to a body no more than half an inch thick.

He still wore the clothes Jake had seen him in last, but now they shapelessly hugged what was left of Rob's formless body. Sweat stains crusted the underarms of his shirt in sagging yellow half-moons and, with no neck for the collar to grasp, it hung limp, exposing the brown ring running along the inside.

The skin of Rob's arms and face was wrinkled and stiff like beef jerky, so dry Jake could see where flakes had broken off like the outer edges of a scab. As horrific as the scene was, Jake couldn't help but notice it was the first time he'd ever seen the man not moistened with sweat from head to toe, and the thought made him smile in spite of it.

Rob was no more than a dry, empty sack whose bones decided to jump ship and strike out on their own, and yet the phone on his desk continued to ring like he was going to pick up the receiver any second. Jake was positive the crunchy husk of his former supervisor wasn't going to fly across the desk and wrap itself around him, but he still approached slowly, keeping his eyes locked on the leather sack just in case.

He stood on the other side of the desk and waited a few seconds until deciding he could trust Rob to stay put. Then, he reached across the desk, lifted the receiver from its cradle, and brought it to his ear.

"Hello?"

"Jacob," said a voice Jake knew right away was Tim's. "Why are you at the old facility? I thought Max told you to go home and wait for him to call you?"

"W—What?" Jake stammered through clenched teeth. "What the hell is going on?"

He wanted to sound more demanding and come off tougher than he actually was, but he lacked the capacity to fall into character at the moment.

"I wish you would have just gone home," Tim said.

"What did you do to Rob? Where did you take Paris? Why—Why the hell are you in all these old pictures?"

"Go home. Wait for Max to call, and we'll sort this out first thing Monday morning."

"The hell we will!"

He shouted into the receiver having suddenly regained the ability to do so, but Tim had hung up, leaving the wailing dial tone to answer for him. Jake slammed the receiver down onto the base, and the force tipped over the small cafeteria table Rob used for a desk. The stack of papers and several pens next to the phone scattered across the office floor already littered with empty coffee cups and crumpled sheets of paper.

With the table out of the way, Jake could see the lower half of his former supervisor's body and what had become of it. The closer his pants got to his ankles, the more entangled they became in the empty, dry flesh of his legs. His shoes lay at either side of the chair, and what poured from the bottom of Rob's pants hardly resembled feet anymore.

The skin had joined together and twisted downward in a single braid that got tighter the closer it came to the floor. And no, it wasn't just touching the floor; it was going through it. There was what looked like random lines burned in the floor around the entry point of Rob's fused feet, but there was nothing random about them for Jake.

A moment later he was sprinting down the hall, following the light from the thankfully still open door. If he wanted to find Max and Paris he would have to go back to the main facility, and go there a hell of a lot sooner than Monday morning. First, he needed to stop back at his apartment for the book of campaigns for Mage of the Hellmouth he'd found before Paris called.

The lines burned in the floor of Rob's office came together in the shape of a symbol Jake recognized right away because it was fresh on his mind. It was the same symbol the Mage wore on his robe, as depicted on the cover of a game he hadn't played since he was twelve.

22

JAKE STOOD IN THE HALLWAY, glad he hadn't come home when Max told him to. The door to his apartment was on the living room floor, the hinges clinging to chunks of jagged, sharp-angled wood from the frame were evidence they'd held up their part of the deal. It was the wood to which they were attached that had given up.

He poked his head slowly across the threshold of the mangled doorway and glanced around quickly, trying to determine if the person or persons responsible were still inside. The initial glimpse was enough for him to see his place was completely trashed, and he stepped inside to get the full scope.

Jake could now see his apartment wasn't trashed at all because trashed was only cluttered compared to what he was looking at. Nearly every inch of the floor was covered with paper or trash, and the spots that weren't looked like they'd been gouged at and burned.

The comforter and sheets had been pulled from the mattress and shredded into long, mangled strips now hanging from light fixtures or lying randomly across the floor like forgotten streamers thrown at a surprise party.

The mattress was torn into as well, having expelled cotton tumbleweeds in all sizes that rolled lazily back and forth across the room, riding the draft from the permanently open door. The nightstand was on its side and, while he couldn't immediately see it, Jake assumed the new phone wouldn't be in working order. He stepped in farther, until he could see around the corner into the kitchen.

The door to the refrigerator mocked him from where it lay on the floor surrounded by what paltry contents came from within, residing in various stages of destruction. The floor was sticky from beer and maple syrup, and broken glass crunched beneath Jake's foot before sticking to the bottom of his shoe.

Every drawer had been pulled from its place beneath the counter and left overturned on the floor before the gaping, empty space left in its absence. Silverware, spatulas, and other utensils were strewn carelessly across the kitchen in the way an impatient child would toss sprinkles on a sundae they couldn't eat soon enough.

The boxes Jake pulled from the closet while looking for Mage of the Hellmouth had been tossed over, spilling condensed segments of his childhood into small, concentrated piles. The boxes he'd left in the closet now lay amongst the rest, upside down and empty, the treasures they'd held now dumped out and flung away.

Jake kicked remnants of broken beer bottles and other unidentifiable trash to the side as he made his way to the approximate area the campaign book *should* be, but the overwhelming vibe of loss circulating the apartment wouldn't let him be hopeful. He picked up some of the boxes and tossed them to the side so his view of the floor was unobstructed.

He crouched in a catcher's stance and gently pushed aside old magazines and comic books now ripped and ruined, being careful not to cut his fingers on any hidden slivers of broken glass. Everything he touched was sticky, but not from spilled beer and the various sundry condiments and syrup coating the kitchen floor. This substance was thicker and viscous with a slick, wet feel rather than the messy, random concoction he'd stepped through in front of the refrigerator.

He rubbed some between his thumb and forefinger and, when he pulled them apart, a thin, clear strand was attached at each end. He wiped his hand on his jeans and continued rummaging to distract from the thundercloud of panic swelling to a monsoon in his chest.

Underneath some fabric shreds torn from Jake's sheets and half of a yearbook from his junior year he found what was left of some campaign books from the various role-playing games he'd played to death with his friends. The excitement of being on the right track tickled his stomach like tiny lightning strikes rebelling from the impending panic storm.

Much like actual lightning, the feeling faded quickly as Jake searched deeper through the stack, unable to find Mage of the Hellmouth. He stood to give his knees a break and ran his hands back through his hair in frustration. The frustration turned to fiery anger when he realized his hands were covered in the damp, sticky mystery all over the floor, and now it was in his hair.

He clenched his fists and tried to breathe away the panic but, at this point, it was like blowing on a forest fire. Jake didn't know what the book would tell him, if anything, or what he would even do if it did. For all he knew, this could be a waste of time, time he could be using to find Max and Paris.

"MOTHERFUCKING SHIT!"

Jake kicked the pile he'd been rifling through and screamed louder than he'd ever screamed before, except when he went to see Van Halen. The difference being this came from a very dark and different place, like he'd tapped into a hidden sub-vocal chamber located beneath his stomach.

He bent over with his hands on his knees to catch his breath and panted through tears for over a minute before his eyes cleared up enough for him to see it. On the floor in front of him was a single page torn from the Mage of the Hellmouth book that had been buried somewhere beneath the pile he kicked away.

On the page was a drawing corresponding to a campaign in the book it was torn from. It was colorful and detailed and drawn in the standard fantasy-style found in role-playing games and on covers of cheap grocery store paperbacks involving unicorns. He picked up the page, walked out from the center of the trash pile, and stood by the window.

In the foreground was the three-headed dog known as Cerberus who legendarily guards the gates of Hell to keep the dead from escaping. The body of the beast loomed large on the jagged crag it stood upon, striking an intimidating posture with an impossible amount of bulging muscle to back it up.

The mouths of each head were curled back into snarls, filled to overflowing with fangs that pulverized as well as they pierced. Ropey, long strands of bloody drool hung from their wicked jowls like frothy tinsel stuck to a tree left in the street long after the holiday had passed. It might have been just his impression, but Jake could see hate and malevolence in the six black eyes regardless of whether or not the artist intended it to be there.

The particular detail that stood out the most to Jake was the red rope looped around the neck of each head. The individual ropes trailed only a short distance behind the mammoth guardian of Hell before twisting together into a single, long length of red rope.

Jake's eyes followed the rope to a cliff above Cerberus, where it was being held tightly in the Mage's right hand. Three knots were tied into the rope along the length of it. His left hand was thrust into the air where a burning pentagram in his palm was backlit by a swirl of glittery iridescence. This was meant to signify the power the Mage possessed now that he controlled the three-headed titan. Beneath the drawing, written in stylized script, was the name of the campaign:

Subduing the Heads of Cerberus

Jake moved closer to the window and saw not even the ashtray filled with roaches he kept on the sill had been spared in the melee of destruction. Chunks of broken glass were strewn across the windowsill, mixed with green and gray ash like an arts and crafts table from a hippie commune.

He looked at the picture again and glanced up and out the window. Across the river beyond the buildings on the far side of town, the glow from the facility seemed to take dusk hostage, pulling the darkness toward it in order to be more visible. The pink glow had turned a dark crimson that stretched farther into the sky like it was reaching up for something.

Jake didn't realize he'd clenched his fists, inadvertently crumpling the page he'd found from the campaign book. He smoothed it against his leg, quickly folded it haphazardly, and jammed it down into the back pocket of his jeans. He took one more look at the fiery glow in the distance before stomping across the mess his apartment had been turned into and toward the door-less opening.

Jake was a few steps from the door when he found out he wasn't in the apartment alone after all, the realization coming in the form of a blow to the back of the head.

23

WHAT HAD PARENTS UP IN arms against games like Mage of the Hellmouth was the satanic stigma attached by conservative Bible-thumpers who deemed it their responsibility to tell the world why they were going to Hell and what was sending them there. It wasn't just the games they took issue with, but popular music, movies, and books as well. It seemed introducing culture into one's life came saddled with eternal damnation.

There was an endless string of news segments containing footage of steamrollers and other construction equipment destroying piles and piles of records and tapes. Rallies took place during which books were shoveled into giant bonfires while unfortunate looking children sang hymns off-key without any sense of rhythm. A holier-than-thou blowhard leading the charge would be more than willing to spout unsolicited, fear-based justifications into any camera pointed their direction.

The games were a different case and came under a harsher, more specific scrutiny. While heavy metal music may be programming children for evil by way of masked or subliminal messages, the games Jake and his friends played took it a step further. They incorporated actual occult symbols, spells, and related imagery religious zealots claimed were helping children to commune directly with the Devil.

Rumors spread quickly through suburban parents, based on nothing but hearsay, equating to a glorified game of telephone on a massive scale. It started with Dungeons and Dragons being pulled from some of the major toy chains, followed by similar games like

Mage. A few weeks later the games were dropped from all major retailers, and the only place they could be found was in hobby or comic book shops. Even then selection was limited, and it could take months for them to stock fresh campaigns or completely new titles, if any.

Two months later, parents stopped caring about what their children listened to, read, watched, or played, having shifted concern to the next thing they were told was sending them to Hell. The games quietly started to reappear in stores, but the damage had been done, with most kids having lost interest. Soon stores carried only the most mainstream, watered-down versions of the games, which were nowhere near the caliber of their pioneering predecessors.

Jake and his friends actually had no idea how lucky they were to have been among the very few to actually play Mage of the Hellmouth. The game was made by a small, independent, upstart game company called Prognosticative Play, and Mage was the first and only game they released. A limited budget meant only a small run of the game was able to be produced, but they hoped putting all their eggs in Mage's basket would pay off in more than enough profit to produce a second run and design new campaigns.

Unfortunately, the gamble didn't pay off, as their game was released when the religious outcry had reached its frenzied peak, and the bottom dropped out of the entire industry. While the dip in the market lasted only a short time, Prognosticative Play and small companies like them didn't have the resources to survive and folded.

Mage of the Hellmouth was released regionally and only a handful of them ever made it to the shelves. The bulk of the copies were never unboxed, since the stores were no longer carrying them, and then shipped around from place to place until they were eventually destroyed. Of the ones bought, it was unknown how many were purchased to destroy in a satanic panic versus those actually played, but odds were not too many when it came to the latter.

Many of the older, hard to find D&D campaigns were acquired by other companies and re-released with updated artwork and packaging offered along with an updated price. Mage of the Hellmouth, unfortunately, didn't receive such treatment and fell through the cracks to exist only as a faint memory to the few who played.

24

CONSCIOUSNESS SWELLED IN JAKE'S HEAD like a balloon attached to a wide-open spigot that pushed away the lingering darkness to force him awake. The first thing he felt was the cold, a cold he'd been in long enough for it to burrow deep into his midsection.

He felt pressure against his chest and arms pushing in from the outside, keeping him immobile while making it hard to draw deep breaths. The air smelled sweet but stale and, just before he opened his eyes, Jake realized exactly where he was. He was in The Box.

Blurry, black dots with crispy purple edges spun, obscuring circles across his vision before he blinked them back. Jake's surroundings came into focus and, while he was indeed in The Box, some drastic changes had been made to the space.

The lights weren't on but a phantom glow had settled across the room, providing an eerie illumination out of thin air. The ceiling was significantly higher, by twenty feet or more, and the floor was clear of pallets to reveal thick, burnt, black lines. The lines formed a much larger version of the same symbol Jake found branded into the floor beneath his former supervisor turned jerky: the Mage's symbol.

A thin layer of translucent, white fog sat inches above the floor and churned lazily back and forth across the room in rolling tufts of vapor. Jake looked down to see he was sitting in a chair, which he also happened to be tied to, thus explaining the pressure against his chest. His arms were at his sides and useless, being held against his body by the same rope keeping him in the chair. Even in the low glowing light he could tell the rope was red.

Tim stood in front of him, but Jake didn't know if the man just appeared, or had been there before he'd opened his eyes. Tim wore a long robe not dissimilar to what the Mage wore in pictures from different campaigns. Tim's was black, whereas the robe in the game was depicted as a deep red. The hood was up, and Tim lowered it when Jake looked up at him.

The same symbol was drawn on his forehead in what was too wet and too red not to be blood. Despite the length of the robe's sleeves, the knotted, dangling ends of Tim's bracelet peeked from beneath the cuff. Jake released a breath he didn't realize he'd been holding, big enough to create a temporary smokescreen between the two of them.

The foggy vapor wrapped around Tim's head as it dissipated, and the billowy frame made for a lighthearted contradiction to the face within its border. His lips parted like a fresh incision and spread just far enough across his face to look unnatural. Clenched teeth formed a seamless, white gleam to complete the unnatural look.

"Hello, Jacob."

Tim's voice now had a quality to it that somehow turned the cold air around Jake colder, but no steam escaped his mouth when he spoke. The air suddenly became thinner, and Jake gasped quick, short breaths that sent small clouds of vapor floating up past his head like he was sending smoke signals.

"I'm sure I don't have to tell you where you are," continued Tim. "Sorry about sticking you in here by the way, but I needed to be sure. There was a period of time when Ian was considered as a fit, but that was before you'd been transferred to the facility."

"I thought his name was Ivan?"

Jake finally caught enough of his breath to speak, and Tim's smile stretched sickeningly further across his face.

"Ian? Ivan? It doesn't matter anymore, not that it ever did. Especially once you were here."

"What . . . what is th—"

"An explanation is in order. In that, you are correct." Tim reached deep into his left sleeve and came out with a folded piece of paper. "But, I believe you're already vaguely familiar with what is happening."

Tim unfolded the paper and held it up for Jake to see. It was the page he'd found buried amongst the chaos his apartment had been turned into and, suddenly, aspects of the image became startlingly similar to his current surroundings. There was nothing to denote an implied temperature in the picture but, now, instead of interpreting it as smoke rising out from behind the Mage, Jake saw cold fog floating up from the same frigid pit in which he presently resided.

Jake didn't remember Mage of the Hellmouth existed a week ago, but what he'd seen over the last three days dragged the memory from a dark, dead spot in his brain and slapped him in the face with it. The symbol he found burned into the ground in Rob's office and its larger counterpart on the floor in front of him currently played a substantial part in sparking the recovered memory, but not by itself. The combination of the red bracelets, the dog-headed Elise, *and* the symbol combined brought it all back around for him.

"That's a drawing from a game," Jake said, a slight edge creeping into his tone. "What does a *stupid* game have to do with you, or me, or this fucked up ice cream factory, if that's even what you've been making this whole time."

He wasn't scared anymore, as the emotion had alchemized into a growing rage. Tim's smile waned, and the paper he held out between his thumb and forefinger burst into flames but, still, Jake kept fear from reinvading his mindset. The page burned quick like flash-paper and left no trace of ash behind.

"You're right," Tim said after waiting a beat like he was expecting applause for his magic trick. "It is a game, yes, but based on very real events. Some of which have yet to happen."

This wasn't what he expected Tim to say, not that Jake had any pre-formed expectations. If he had, this wouldn't be on the list of hypotheses. Was it possible Tim was some kind of psychopath unable to differentiate between fiction and reality who believed himself to be the titular Mage from Mage of the Hellmouth?

There was something about the way he said *very real events* that was enough to blow apart his quickly cobbled together theory. It held an imperceptible tone that worked like a dog whistle to immediately tame Jake's anger back into fear. Still, he used his last drops of moxie to fire off the final bit of attitude he could muster.

"Don't tell me you're one of those satanic panic assholes ignorant enough to believe heavy metal and role-playing games really hold evil powers. Because honestly, I had you pegged as a sma—"

Tim reached a hand inside his robe, and it came back holding something else Jake recognized—Max's head. It hung from the tightly clenched fistful of hair tangled between Tim's fingers like a prize dangling from the hooks of a claw-machine game. The face, while unmistakably Max, hung slack and featureless like a decommissioned, animatronic president from a theme park.

There was no blood or fluid leaking out, and the eyes were glassy and dry and clouded by death. It was clear the beheading wasn't recent. Jagged, triangular flaps of skin circled the perimeter where the neck had been severed and, judging from the sloppiness of the cut, a dull blade was used.

This development added an entirely new weight to an already incredibly heavy situation. He gulped at mouthfuls of air with as much success as a fish out of water. A floating sensation made Jake feel like his head had come unattached as well and was being lifted by another robe-wearing Satanist to create a macabre, real-life reflection of what he saw.

"Shall I continue, or are there any other opinions you'd like to laud my way?"

Jake still couldn't breathe. He'd somehow lost access to the muscles controlling the function. Either that, or he'd forgotten how to do so entirely. Speaking was completely out of the question.

"As I was saying," Tim continued, slipping the head back into the robe and the phantom zone from which he'd pulled it, "the game you played as a child was more of a prophecy, but a living one. Some aspects were set in stone, but there were other parts that could be manipulated by changing certain variables.

"This served as a way of seeing how different scenarios would play out beforehand, allowing consequences to be weighed against benefits when it came time for actual decisions to be made. There are always some minor variations between prediction and reality that can't be helped, but they've so far proven to be of no consequence."

The weight against his back and chest hadn't subsided, but Jake still fought to manage small gasps into his compressed lungs.

"Who?" Jake's voice came out as a gravelly whisper. "Who made the game? Who is making the choices? Who . . . who are you?"

He pushed as many questions out in the small amount of breath he was able to manage. Tim laughed in halting bursts of sound, creating coinciding vapor clouds to commingle with the chilly fog above his head.

"Simply put, the answer is me."

He waited a beat, as if dragging the moment out was supposed to make things that much more confusing for Jake.

"Do you know what a Cambion is?" Tim didn't pause for an answer, assuming correctly Jake did not know. "There are a few ways to explain it, depending, but the easiest is to say a Cambion is the offspring of a demon and a human. There are different ways in which this is done, varying from case to case.

"Despite *how* it happens, it does. I am a Cambion."

"My father was a demon named Foras," Tim continued. "My mother was a witch called Ingrid, who was the most powerful among her coven and much further advanced in the dark arts than her sisters. But, as it so often goes, she was hungry for more."

Tim started to pace as he told his story, and the air bent around him with each step like the room was breathing.

"She summoned Foras and held him captive within an enchanted circle until he agreed to mate with her, believing this would join them together in a way that allowed her eternal access to his power. He was a president in Hell, and she would be his First Lady."

The room vibrated in time with each step, as if placing emphasis on certain words. Somewhere in the darkness from across the room beyond Tim, Jake heard something dripping. It was soft at first, like the patter rain makes on the sidewalk when the drops are between a drizzle and a downpour. A moment later, it became distinct and steady.

Whatever was making the noise wasn't falling faster, but it had gotten heavier. Jake nearly tuned Tim out completely while focusing on the sound, trying to pinpoint its location.

"Foras had a different idea of how their union would play out. When I was born six days after conception, he ripped my mother to shreds and devoured her soul. He returned to Hell, and I was left to be raised by the coven only because they were afraid of what would happen if they killed me."

A second drip started but sounded like it was off a few feet to the left of the original one. Together they created an offbeat rhythm that worked against the initial timing of the first drip, making for an appropriate dissonance. Jake couldn't tell if it was actually getting brighter or if his eyes had further adjusted, but the darkness appeared to be slowly lifting from the room.

"Being what I was," Tim continued, unaware or uncaring of the change, "I was imbued with abilities that allowed me to take in the dark arts at a rapid rate, and the witches who raised me taught me how to properly and effectively wield my power. Before long I became a finely tuned master sorcerer with the ability to bend reality eternally in my favor, regardless of the situation."

Something else started dripping to the right of the original, even harder and faster, decidedly taking lead in the oddly crafted, percussive, power-groove echoing within The Box.

"This was all well and good, but I wanted more." Tim stopped and leveled his gaze down at Jake. "I wanted what my father had. He was commander over twenty-nine legions of demons and ranked high among the sovereignty of Hell and, while the power I had could provide me almost anything, it couldn't give me what I wanted most.

"I set out to find the Hellmouth, where I intended to march through the blackened gates and claim what I believe is my birthright. Finding the Hellmouth wasn't a challenge, but using it would prove more difficult than I anticipated."

Jake found he was able to draw deeper and longer breaths, but the pressure around him refused to let up. He wasn't imagining the light. The bottom portion of the wall beyond Tim had become obviously brighter. The light worked its way up the wall teasingly, like a call girl lifting up her skirt, making you hold out as long as possible for the "good part."

He could see puddles on the floor being made by the three separate drips. The one in the middle was red while, on either side, they were foamy and tinted yellow. Jake's breathing suddenly turned to short, quick gasps but not because his chest had gotten any tighter. It was a reaction to what he was seeing now that the room was bright enough for him to learn what was making the puddles.

Tim stopped and turned around, following Jake's sightline to see what had put him in such a state. He smiled wide enough to swallow his face and raised his hand as if formally presenting the new horrors to Jake.

Tim paused and turned to look back at Jake, "I trust you've heard of Cerberus."

25

JAKE AND HIS FRIENDS PLAYED through all the campaigns included with Mage of the Hellmouth and, while all were challenging, adding to the overall enjoyment of the game, there was one in particular that proved more difficult than the rest. They attempted it many times and always ended up putting it aside to come back to at another time. The campaign was called "Subduing the Heads of Cerberus."

Each player was on the Mage's side in this campaign, pitting all demons and hell-spawn against the entire group. The ultimate goal was to harness control of Cerberus in order to gain access to Hell while using its great guardian against them. The difficulty came in having to complete each task in a very specific order to give control of each head to the Mage one at a time.

All the while, demons worked to undo any progress made by the players, and one roll of the dice could erase hours of work. It was so frustrating, Jake had to beg his friends to give it one more try even after months had passed since the last time they'd made an attempt. They were quick to remind him of the entire weekend they lost playing the campaign and ending up with nothing to show for it.

Jake didn't need reminding and shared the frustration his friends felt only, rather than deterring, it spurred him on. He wanted to complete the campaign. He needed to. It took a couple weeks of convincing, along with an incentive of allowing each of them one selection apiece from his prized baseball card collection *if* the attempt proved to be another waste of time. Jake's friends accepted the deal with one caveat of their own being, regardless of the outcome, he would never ask them to play the campaign again.

Jake was confident though and gladly accepted their terms. He wouldn't need to ask because *when* they beat it, there would be no need to play again. He knew his friends expected the same results as before and wanted to eliminate the possibility of being roped back in to another game by way of Jake's incessant pleading and bribery.

They started the campaign on a Friday evening in the basement of Jake's house where they usually played. While his fellow players had forgotten some of the specifics, having forcibly wiped the entire experience from their brains, Jake, on the other hand, remembered very well. He'd thought hard about the various choices they'd made prior, along with the possible outcomes, so when he decided to have them collect the three red, knotted ropes first thing, they were puzzled.

Doing this first left them vulnerable, weak, and unarmed, and from all obvious angles, it would lead the entire party to certain death. Of course, his friends were all for it, thinking the game would end much sooner than expected, allowing them to play a different game that wasn't impossible to complete. Jake's friend Greg had brought some newer campaigns for D&D, figuring they'd come in handy if there happened to be a sudden change of plans.

The plans, in fact, did not change, and while they expected to be wiped out quickly following Jake on his fool's errand, they were quite surprised to be not only successful in finding the rope, but by gaining an advantage in doing so. His friends hadn't seen the angle the last times they'd played, but now it seemed so obvious they didn't know how they'd ever missed it.

The ropes were needed for the Mage to control each head of the Cerberus, individually at first, and then all together as one. The knots gave the rope specific enchantments pertaining to each head, not only giving the Mage control over it, but also imbuing him with the powers each head possessed.

In past attempts, their strategy had been to go for the heads first to try and contain them, and then send someone separately out to find the ropes. The resources they exhausted getting started were what had always put them at a disadvantage. This time they were able to approach things differently, with more time to strategize and weigh each option.

By Saturday evening, the campaign was complete, with Jake and his friends having successfully helped the Mage subdue the Cerberus, become far more powerful than he'd ever been, and launch a siege against Hell to further sate the warlock's lust for power.

Satisfied, Jake put The Mage of the Hellmouth away, and the group spent the rest of the weekend playing Greg's fresh Dungeons and Dragons campaigns. They never mentioned it but Jake could tell his friends felt the same pride and accomplishment as he did. They would never bring it up though, especially not after they'd been so vehement in their initial resistance, but as far as he was concerned, they didn't have to.

Completing the final campaign gave Jake a sense of satisfaction he carried with him long after that weekend and even well beyond after he'd stopped playing games and lost touch with his group of friends. The satisfaction stayed with Jake throughout his whole life, although he never actively thought about it. The feeling morphed into a sense of confidence that continued to serve him well.

Jake learned to not give up on something because it was difficult. He learned not to quit. He learned he *could* do what he put his mind to. These lessons had instilled qualities in Jake that helped form him into the person he'd become, but now he wished he'd never learned them at all.

26

WITH THE ADDITION OF LIGHT, it was clear the ceiling was much higher now than when Jake had been working earlier in the week. There were many things different about The Box now. Platforms previously hidden by shadow were visible suspended twenty feet in the air, floating autonomously, attached to nothing.

Standing on the platforms was what caused Jake to lose his breath again and re-solidified his terror, wrapping spindly, piercing thorns up and into the base of his spine. The sight of what was hanging from the ceiling between the platforms yanked a sickening pain up from his testicles, settling just below his stomach to commiserate with the sharp spikes of terror.

On either platform stood a woman, nude from the neck down, with the head of a snarling, black-eyed dog, their mouths open to show off the unimaginable amount of barbed, razor fangs contained within. Slimy, yellow froth hung from the panting jowls and poured from the sides of their mouths down to the floor, creating two of the three puddles. Around each of their necks was a thick, red rope tied with two different knots.

The dog-headed woman on the left was Elise, and while he instantly recognized the second woman from her body alone, he couldn't convince himself to believe it. It was Paris. He shouldn't have been able to tell it was her but he could. Jake had never seen his best friend's sister naked before, but they'd all been swimming together countless times where Paris wore bikinis that left little to the imagination.

He'd fantasized about one day having intimate exchanges with-her but never could have imagined her form being revealed to him in such an ugly and joyless fashion. Not to mention whoever or whatever Jake was looking at wasn't Paris anymore.

Between the dog-headed women, a body hung upside down from the ceiling with legs spread wide, attached by silver twine wrapped around each ankle. The arms hung slack and swollen where the blood had collected, creating a look of grotesque, disproportionate musculature.

The body was male, but instead of having a dog head it had no head at all. The red puddle flanked by venomous drool was blood leaking from Max's decapitated body.

"I'm sure your mind is swimming with theories."

Jake broke from the spell of what he was seeing and looked back down to see Tim now holding red ropes in his hand. The lengths of which led up to the necks of the dog-headed women. Jake couldn't remember if the ropes appeared in Tim's hand or if he'd been holding them the whole time to maintain control over the brutal power he'd harnessed.

"It's not as complicated as you might think," Tim continued. "Every person who bought and played Mage of the Hellmouth was supposed to. Nothing about it was chance or happenstance. The copies meant to be played went to the person or persons meant to play them. The rest were always meant to remain hidden away in boxes in backs of storerooms until being eventually destroyed, never to see the light of day.

"I cast a spell binding me to the games so I could experience it being played each time it was. I took in hundreds upon hundreds of scenarios played out by those I'd chosen, and it helped to prepare and formulate my attack. It gave me the space to take my time, grow stronger, and continue to strategize, but it was you who added the final missing piece."

"So what?" Jake spat the words, not sure if they would come, but glad when they did. "What are you saying, this is my fault? I'm the reason this happened?"

The vapor accompanying each word out of Jake's mouth seemed to match his frustration with the soft, flowing curves now turned boxy with sharp edges. Tim waited until the clouds thinned and floated up past his face before continuing.

"While I admire your narcissism, I am afraid not. You played a part, yes, but a very small part of a whole that required many, many parts. What I learned from you holds a slight significance only because it was the *last* piece, and for that you shall be rewarded."

The glow illuminating the room grew brighter still, showing Jake what was on the wall behind the platforms holding the dog-headed women. What was left of the dried-out, stiff figures who had been his co-workers were nailed to the wall by large spikes driven into each one of their chests, with Ivan's wilted form directly in the center. His limbs were twisted like a wrung out chamois turned hard and prickly from the sun.

"What you have been experiencing while working for Fam-Mark has essentially been the front I created until the time was right to subdue Cerberus and storm Hell to retrieve my birthright. And it just so happens," Tim paused and looked at a watch on his wrist that wasn't there. "The right time is now."

27

WHEN THE MAGE SET OUT to find the Hellmouth, it wasn't long before he'd discovered the foul, black opening, but he knew better than to think his task would be easy. His lineage, mixed with the teaching and guidance of the coven that raised him, gave the Mage a bevy of powerful and unique abilities.

He entered a deep meditative state where he was able to separate his soul from his body, thereby tricking the psychopomps into guiding his lost spirit to the afterlife for which it was destined. The Mage allowed his soul to be led all the way to the entrance of Hell and just beyond before yanking his soul through the astral plane back into his body.

Upon having learned where to begin, the Mage collected supplies he would need, including several sacred magic tomes he forcibly liberated from the coven's library, as well as a horde of ingredients with which to work the powerful magic he'd need to gain access to Leviathan's pit. These were intended for communal use by the entire coven and, while it provided a major setback, they were relieved to be finally rid of the Mage.

He traveled for weeks to get to where his soul had been prematurely guided to Hell and, upon arriving, wasted no time setting up a small shelter where he would toil endlessly over spells meant to grant him the access he desired. He opened the ground by breaking six magic seals with a long forgotten ancient sigil lost long ago on purpose to prevent it from ever being used. This was the last easy task the Mage would face on a quest that lasted hundreds of years.

When the sixth and final seal was breached, an intense cold

pushed up and out of the opening, plunging the surrounding area into an arctic wasteland. This wasn't a surprise to the Mage, who had been sure to fashion a charm, which he ingested to protect him from the frigid temperature.

While most people took Dante's *Inferno* as a morbid fever dream transcribed by the writer while composing the tale in exile, it was not a dream from which he culled his material. Trapped in the center of Hell was a manifestation known as Satan who actually did flap his wings eternally to create the frosty winds Dante spoke of, but the icy effects weren't contained strictly within the ninth and final circle.

All of Hell was chilled from the center out because of this. The stories of the lake of fire and burning for your sins were just that—stories. Hell was, in actuality, a frozen ball of eternal misery and suffering.

The Mage used every bit of the power and resources available to traverse the many obstacles between the Hellmouth and the actual gates of Hell, but it was there he was met with ultimate adversity in the form of a three-headed beast charged with guarding the unholy entrance. The Mage was forced to retreat back to the surface so he could strategize and better plan his attack.

It took countless tries over many years before the idea of the game came to him, but it didn't start out as a game. There was a long and difficult trial and error period where he used imps he'd conjured or villagers he'd kidnapped to actually attempt the Mage's theories on conquering Cerberus. This was neither effective nor practical, but it allowed him to collect the data he would later use to create Mage of the Hellmouth.

None of these things happened overnight though and, as time passed, the Mage was forced to adapt to changes that came with the progressing years. He constructed several different structures to contain the Hellmouth, suited to reflect the culture of society at the time.

The buildings served no purpose other than to protect the Hellmouth and were plain and unassuming until rapid modernization forced the Mage to be creative in how he hid the entrance to Hell. He obtained a deed to the land and made it appear as if an actual business was being run in the location that would mysteriously shut down directly after opening to avoid suspicion.

With no cars around the building, no business records, and absolutely no comings and goings of any sort, it wouldn't be long before someone came poking around to see what was what. This was why every three months, like clockwork, a new sign appeared over the door, followed promptly by a slightly different looking "Out of Business" sign to replace the previous one.

When strategy based role-playing games started to come around, the Mage very quickly saw the relation to his own arduous quest. It was becoming harder for him to kidnap or lure people in to be used as his personal lab rats even with his vast access to magic. Somewhere along the line people started actually caring when someone went missing and would look for them using all kinds of modern investigative tools humans were inventing.

Operating in this way meant it was only a matter of time before one of his guinea pigs was tracked to the building, jeopardizing hundreds of years of work and carefully crafted preparation. He was going to have to find another way to run his scenarios, and the invention and subsequent rise in popularity of games like Dungeons and Dragons gave the Mage an idea of how to do just that.

For a short time, the sign over the door read Prognosticative Games, where the first actual product was produced in a long line of the Mage's faux businesses, but once the final box of the first run left the loading dock, the "Out of Business" sign was back up. Before that, the Mage placed an enchantment upon the games to put them into specific people's hands.

He didn't know who they were yet, but his spell would keep those who would be of no help from obtaining a copy. The kind of magic the Mage could wield was more than just what made things happen for him. It was a living, sentient energy he used to feel through the collective consciousness and connect himself to those who played the game. There was a certain way of thinking amongst those chosen not shared by many with a particular focus around the deconstruction of things.

Through his magical link to the game, he soaked in all he could from the chosen players' choices and strategies. He started to use the collective data, almost immediately seeing where he had already gone wrong, how he could correct the moves he'd already made, and what to do next to ensure swift and decisive victory.

Even with all the information coming to the Mage so rapidly he was still missing a crucial step, only he didn't know what exactly it was until Jacob Bowman played his final game of Mage of the

Hellmouth. With the last piece needed to launch his attack now in place, the battle for the Mage's entry into Hell was officially underway.

Jacob wasn't the only one who provided crucial insight to the Mage's quest, which was what prompted the start of the Fam-Mark Corporation. Finding the red rope first was the key to it all, giving him control over the employees. He started it as an ice cream business to better help hide the Hellmouth in plain sight.

There were no fans or air-conditioners to keep the room they called The Box cool. The eternal frozen exhale of the open Hellmouth provided the proper temperature to store his product. The best part was they weren't making ice cream at the facility. They weren't actually making anything at all. It was an intricate farce set up for the Mage to control the herd of human cattle required for his success.

Attaching strands of the red rope to his employees using a specific knot allowed him to feed their life energy into the nightly ritual ceremonies the Mage conducted to weaken the heads of Cerberus one at time until he was able to overtake it. Unknowingly, Jake had participated in the last of these ceremonies while working in The Box. The pattern with which he was instructed to place the pallets formed sigils that worked in conjunction with the hidden symbol on the floor.

It wasn't just the arrangement of the pallets but the contents that made the Mage's magic work, and those contents were the concentrated energy he'd sucked from the spellbound Fam-Mark employees. As far as helping the Mage went, Jake had cast the final die that put everything in place, just like he had as a child when he forced his friends to give Mage of the Hellmouth one more try.

The other facility, the one Jake and Max originally worked in, served as nothing but a holding pen for the last of the livestock he'd need to tap into when the time came. If asked, Jake would say he made ice cream at the facility five days a week, but he wouldn't be able to remember how he did it. He wouldn't be able to recall where the ingredients went into the machines or what the ingredients even were.

The truth was, Jake never made any ice cream, or loaded a machine, or even operated one. He only thought he had because that was how the magic worked. Because of the game, the Mage knew what to do, but it didn't mean he could do it fast. It took as long as it was going to take, so Tim kept Jake, Max, Rob, and the rest of the employees together until he needed them.

All day they would stand at their assigned stations in a trance, not doing anything while left to believe they were working hard helping the company to be successful. It was some of the Mage's finest work, as far as he was concerned, but only up until then. He knew there would be no limit to what he could achieve once he'd penetrated the gates and was bestowed with his father's unholy powers. His best work was yet to come.

28

"W—WHY ME?" JAKE STAMMERED through clenched teeth as his pain could no longer block out the cold. "Why did you save me for last?"

The smile returned to Tim's face, cutting the same wide slit from one ear to the other. His hand clutched tightly the red ropes attached to the snarling, dog-headed women, and he flexed his fingers without compromising the strength of his grip.

"I already told you," he sneered, "there is nothing special about you. Nothing at all! My only reasoning behind it is you made the last contribution, so you're last in line to receive your reward."

"Reward? Is that what *they* all received?" Jake gestured his chin up at the empty skins of his coworkers.

"Well," Tim chuckled, "I suppose *that* is more of a punishment than a reward, but you're not destined for the same fate as your coworkers."

"What about Max? Is that the kind of reward you have in store for me?"

"Max," he paused. "Max was the final sacrifice required, and unfortunately for him it was the most invasive one."

"I would say decapitation is a little more than just invasive."

The Mage threw his head back suddenly and laughed loud and long like he'd rehearsed the reaction for just such an occasion, or even specifically for this one. The skin on his face pulled up and out at his cheekbones, which pushed his chin out, emphasizing the point at the end. When the laughter stopped, he lowered his gaze, and Jake saw the contorting of the Mage's features remained in this gruesome state.

He'd become a hideous caricature of himself. A purple tint bloomed beneath his skin like a swirling, living bruise unnaturally darkening his complexion. The Mage's red-rimmed, jaundice-yellow eyes popped against the contrast like two lonely life preservers floating along dark sea water.

His already exaggerated and monstrous teeth appeared longer and sharper through the nightmarish snarl fixed to his transformed face. Thick saliva coated the fangs and dripped from the corner of his cackling maw in slow motion. The laughing continued but, much like the Mage's appearance, was now drastically altered.

The sharp, barked tones it became were at a frequency that riled the dog-headed women into howling at offset pitches. The dissonance yanked at the base of Jake's bowels with sonic fishhooks vigorously working to trigger release. The platforms the dog-headed women stood on shook beneath their frenzy, and the symbol on the floor glowed a deep blood red.

The sporadic bursts of vapor catapulted from the Mage's mouth told Jake it was still cold, only he couldn't feel it anymore. A pea-sized pain started somewhere deep in the center of his brain and became all he could focus on. Even the trio's piercing bark faded far into the background until it was gone completely.

The tiny pain began to swell, overtaking the entire temporal lobe while edging farther out into other parts of his brain. The spread was slow but steady, and soon it outgrew his brain to form a hard shell of agony around it. The shell then started to constrict, causing an indescribable sensation he knew was pain, but Jake couldn't process it correctly. It was possible the part of his brain needed to decipher this particular code had already been damaged by the tremendous pressure bearing down on all sides.

Jake was never one to consider his mortality, but for the first time it was becoming clear he would not make it through whatever the hell was happening to him alive. The continuous constriction pushed farther inward, rupturing sections of his brain while the damage robbed Jake of his faculties one at a time.

His vision faded into faraway pinpoints through which he saw the Mage close his mouth, ceasing the wretched laughter, and as the last puff of breath faded away, so did Jake.

29

HE FELT THE COLD IN the tip of his nose first as the nerve receptors came back online. The sensation moved out to the sides of his face beneath his eyes and settled into the rubbery, pliable cartilage of his ears. A second later his entire body lit up at once like someone plugged in the lights on a Christmas tree. Jake clenched his teeth against their involuntary chatter and slowly opened his eyes.

His vision was blurred and foggy like the windshield of a car in winter and, using his eyelids as wipers, he attempted to blink it clear. The act emulated the effect of turning the defroster on, clearing the obstructive blur starting at the edges and working in toward the center. Soon Jake could see the Mage standing in front of him clear as day.

Whatever effects the strangely pitched laughter/barking/howling had on him only lasted for the short duration it was emitted. No time had passed, but Jake felt beat up, sore, and strangely old, like a lifetime had gone by since closing his eyes and opening them again. Everything inside him wanted to stop, to let go of consciousness or life, whichever came first.

"I know, I know," the Mage said. His voice had changed along with his face and now sounded like his vocal cords had been used as a scratching post for feral cats. "The pain was, well . . . I would say exquisite, but I'm sure you would choose different ways of describing it."

Jake could only respond in long, hot breaths of vapor threatening to fog over his vision again. His eyes felt dry and tacky like wet paint, unable to stay well lubricated in the extreme temperature.

"Not that it matters," continued the Mage. "The pain you're destined for will have you longing for what you just went through as a brief respite, but there won't be one. You will be reformed in energy solely comprised of such pain that you will forever be chasing death."

Jake made an attempt at speaking again, resulting in a whispery groan playing more like a slow exhale than verbal communication. He tried to rest his head back against whatever he was tied to but something tugged at his neck, holding him in place. He glanced down and saw a length of red rope tied around his neck, the end of which was held tightly in the Mage's hand with the others.

He thought maybe the rope had been tied around his neck the entire time, but the look in the Mage's eyes told Jake it was most likely a recent addition to his bonds. Of course it was, though. The Mage was savoring the final moments leading up to his victory, sucking the marrow greedily from each discarded bone. He didn't want to tip his hat by having Jake realize how absolutely and utterly fucked he was right from the start. He needed to draw it out, if even only for a short time.

He'd planned the structure of the entire reveal and knew exactly how each wrinkle would unfold. From Jake's recognition of being in The Box, to the lights rising slowly to show first the blood and drool, then the dog-headed women with the beheaded Max hung between them, and finally the husks of his co-workers unceremoniously nailed to the wall. All of it went exactly as the Mage planned.

"The rope was the key the whole time," the Mage's eyes began to glow as he spoke. "The red rope. I knew it too. I just wasn't going about things in the correct order until you showed me where to start. I always knew where I was going, and I found out exactly how to get there, but regardless of what I did I couldn't make it all work until I started from the right spot.

"I was able to easily bend the first head to my will shortly thereafter, and then it was just a matter of taking time to execute the rest of the steps, all of which were lined out for me thanks to Mage of the Hellmouth."

From the platforms above, what used to be Elise and Paris began to stir with anxiety like dogs in a thunderstorm. Whatever it was they were feeling, Jake felt it too. Their growling was more like aggressive purring than any sound a dog would make.

"And now, as I prepare to breach the Hellmouth on my way to

certain victory, your *reward* is to be with me not only on the front lines but for always as one-third of my own personal enforcer."

Images of retch-inducing acts of violence flashed through Jake's mind from the past, present, and somehow the future. Most so deplorable he could only register them as subjective works of impressionistic art because surely nothing like what he was seeing could be real. It made more sense for them to have been concocted from the twisted and eternally depressed state of mind expected in a tortured artist rather than a snapshot from Jake's waking reality.

The friction of the rope grew abruptly snug around his neck, but Jake quickly realized it wasn't getting tighter, it was getting hotter.

"Congratulations, Jacob, here is your reward!"

Jake's face exploded. The underside pushed out suddenly and quickly, as if having launched a sneak attack on the unsuspecting dermis. It wasn't a case of muscle outgrowing its skin casing like an overstuffed sausage. The shape of his head was changing as well.

His skull pushed out from the center of, what was seconds ago, his face, elongating Jake's upper and lower jaw with it. The ligaments on the right side of his face snapped, causing the bulging musculature to detach from the changing skull beneath and flap off to the left like it was a page turning in a book. It hung from the base of his ear, sloppy and formless like old, wet beef left in the butcher shop window too long.

The bone of Jake's elongating jaw cracked like a chorus of crab legs being plundered at a cheap seafood buffet as fangs forced their way into their new home in his mouth. The limp meat of his old face fell to the cold floor with a slap like ham on a skillet. New muscle, skin and hair raised itself across the new face from one side to the other, a layer at a time like time-lapse footage of a skyscraper being built.

There were a few moments when Jake couldn't see because skin and muscle were bunched up over his eyes while what was beneath continued rearranging itself. As he blinked through freshly formed eyelids, he could see the Mage still standing there holding the three red ropes, but something was different about the way he was seeing it.

Everything seemed somehow sharper and crisper, and he could see every detail despite the distance from him. His vision suddenly became so powerful it was like he was somehow able to see around walls, past doorways, through time and dimensional dividers. Jake saw everything and nothing at once with a multitude of scenarios, all of which he already knew the outcome to.

The sound of a buzz saw came from far away, getting closer until it sat perched at the opening of his ear as if waiting for permission to enter. By that time, Jake realized the sound wasn't coming from outside and far away. It was coming from him. Jake was growling but he wasn't really Jake anymore, not completely, at least.

He didn't know when he'd been untied, but he must have been because he was standing now and moving toward the Mage. Not walking but floating or, at least Jake assumed since he couldn't feel anything below his neck. A moment later he knew he was floating. He watched the Mage grow smaller with his ascent. The Cambion warlock threw his head back and cackled madly, only now the sound wasn't offensive to his ears.

Jake heard the dog-headed women join in right on cue a moment before he looked up to see them floating toward him, sounding their atonal howl. He wasn't afraid, and he wasn't in pain. The choral dissonance became thicker and more distinct with the addition of Jake's own torturous wail.

Elise, Paris, and Jake came together at the center of the room directly above the Mage, and the three became one amidst the simultaneous climax of their combined bray. The symbol on the floor glowed brighter and brighter, and suddenly Jake was part of something more powerful and important than he would have been able to fathom.

Jake gave himself willingly to the culminating energies and let what was left of him be swallowed by the churning darkness until there was nothing left at all.

ACKNOWLEDGEMENTS

Special thanks to Grindhouse Press, Roy, Kris, and my drug dealer(s).

John Wayne Comunale lives in Houston Texas to prepare himself for the heat in Hell. He is the author of books such as *Death Pacts and Left-Hand Paths, Scummer, As Seen On T.V., Sinkhole, The Cycle* and more. He hosts three weekly podcasts, fronts the punk rock disaster, johnwayneisdead, and travels around the country giving truly unique performances of the written word. John Wayne was an American actor who died in 1979.

Other Grindhouse Press Titles